POPPY & SAM
AND THE SEARCH FOR SLEEP

By CATHON

Translated by Susan Ouriou

Owlkids Books

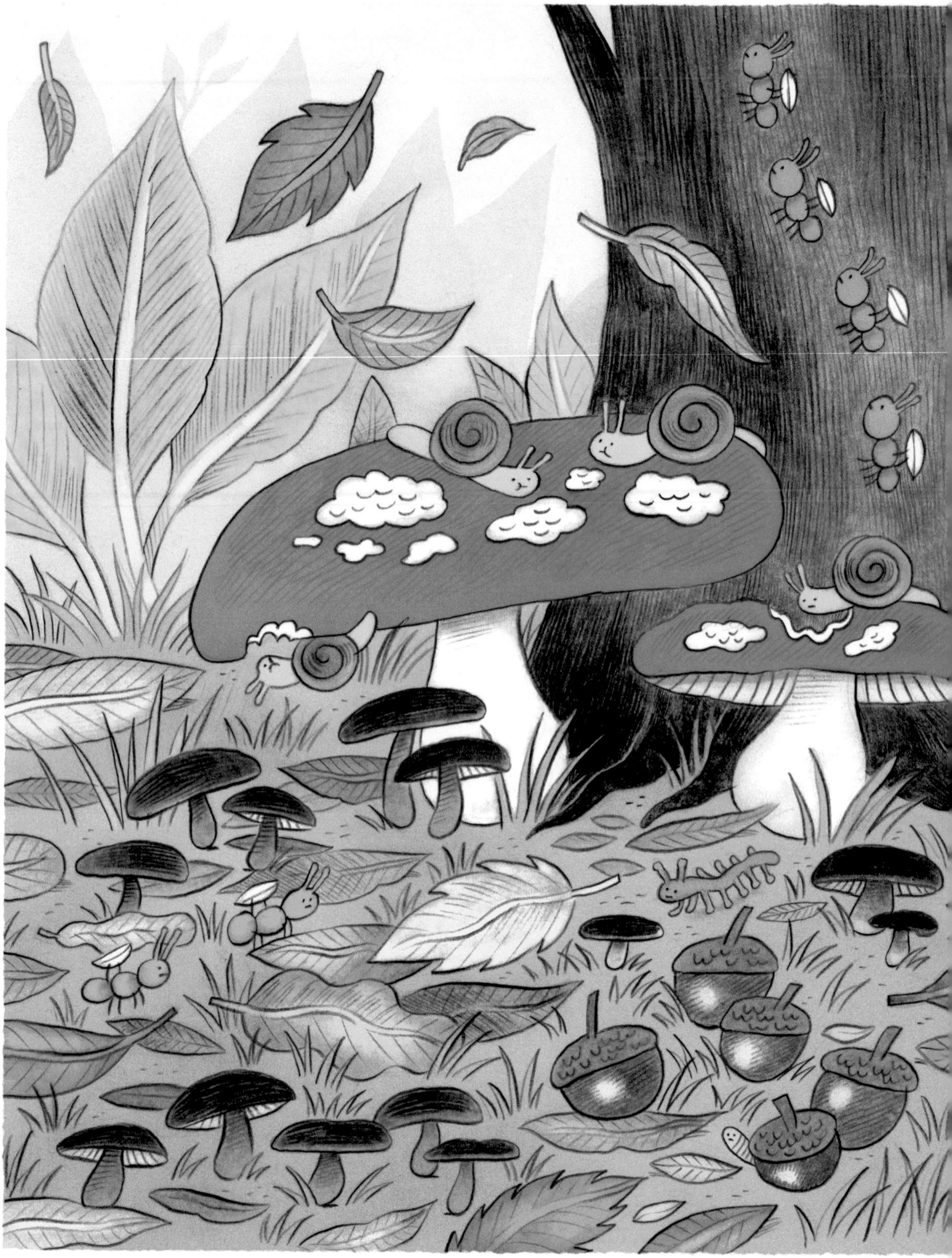

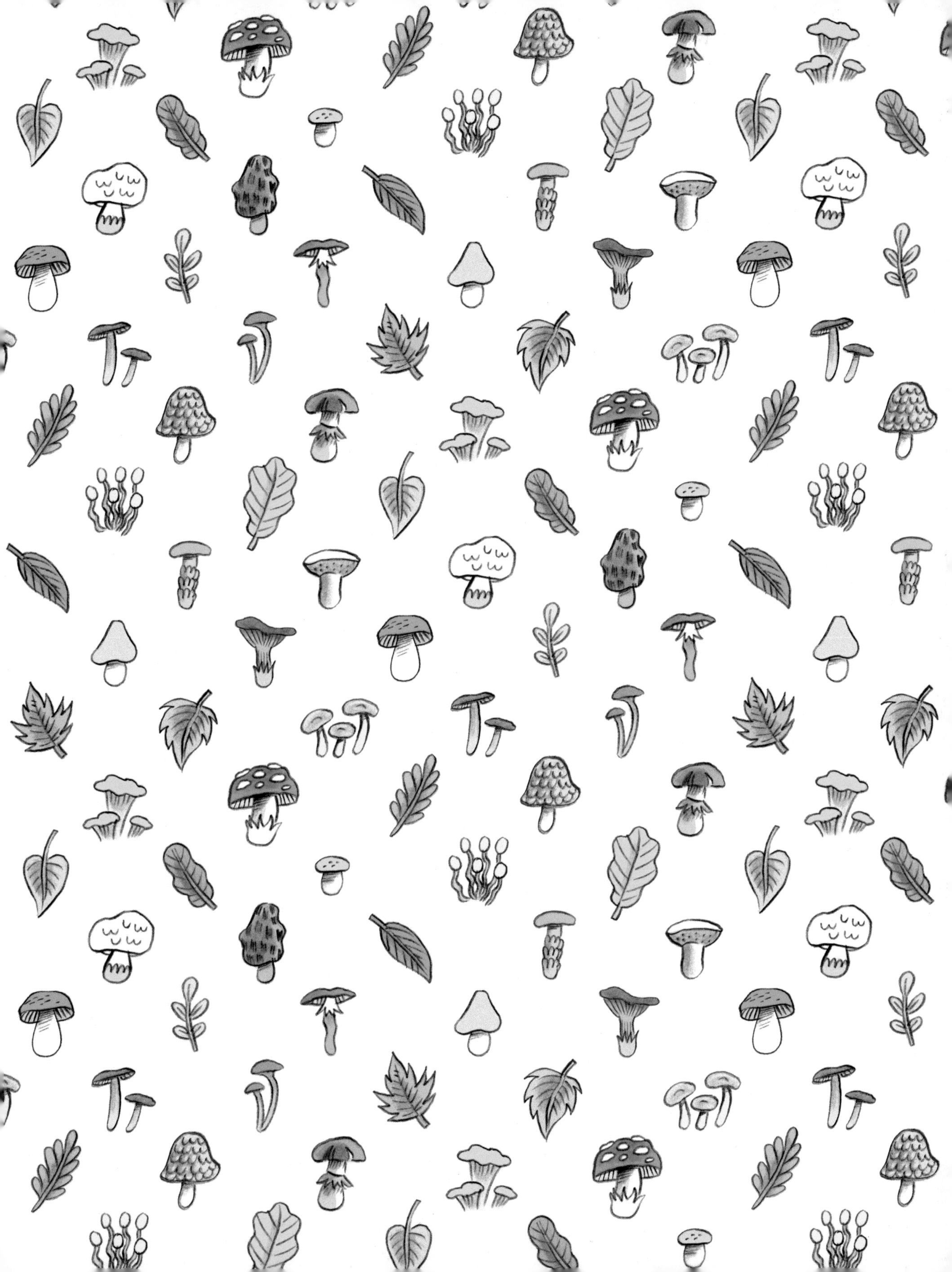

For Iris, my favorite night owl

First edition 2020
Originally published under the title *Mimose & Sam : Mission hibernation*
Published with the permission of Comme des géants inc.,
38, rue Sainte-Anne, Varennes, Québec, Canada J3X 1R5

Translation rights arranged through the VeroK Agency, Barcelona, Spain

Published in English in 2020 by Owlkids Books Inc.

Owlkids Books acknowledges the financial support of the Canada Council for the Arts, the Ontario Arts Council, the Government of Canada through the Canada Book Fund (CBF), and the Government of Ontario through the Ontario Creates Book Initiative for our publishing activities.

Published in Canada by
Owlkids Books Inc.
1 Eglinton Avenue East
Toronto, ON M4P 3A1

Published in the United States by
Owlkids Books Inc.
1700 Fourth Street
Berkeley, CA 94710

Library and Archives Canada Cataloguing in Publication

Title: Poppy & Sam and the search for sleep / by Cathon ; translated by Susan Ouriou.
Other titles: Mimose et Sam, mission hibernation. English | Poppy and Sam and the search for sleep | Search for sleep
Names: Cathon, 1990- author, illustrator. | Ouriou, Susan, translator.
Description: Translation of: Mimose et Sam, mission hibernation.
Identifiers: Canadiana 20200178504 | ISBN 9781771474184 (hardcover)
Subjects: LCGFT: Picture books.
Classification: LCC PS8605.A8786 M5613 2020 | DDC jC843/.6—dc23

Library of Congress Control Number: 2020930801

ONTARIO ARTS COUNCIL
CONSEIL DES ARTS DE L'ONTARIO
an Ontario government agency
un organisme du gouvernement de l'Ontario

Canada Council for the Arts
Conseil des Arts du Canada

Canada

Manufactured in Shenzhen, Guangdong, China, in May 2020, by WKT Co. Ltd.
Job #19CB2648

A B C D E F

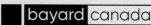

Publisher of Chirp, Chickadee and OWL
www.owlkidsbooks.com

Owlkids Books is a division of bayard canada

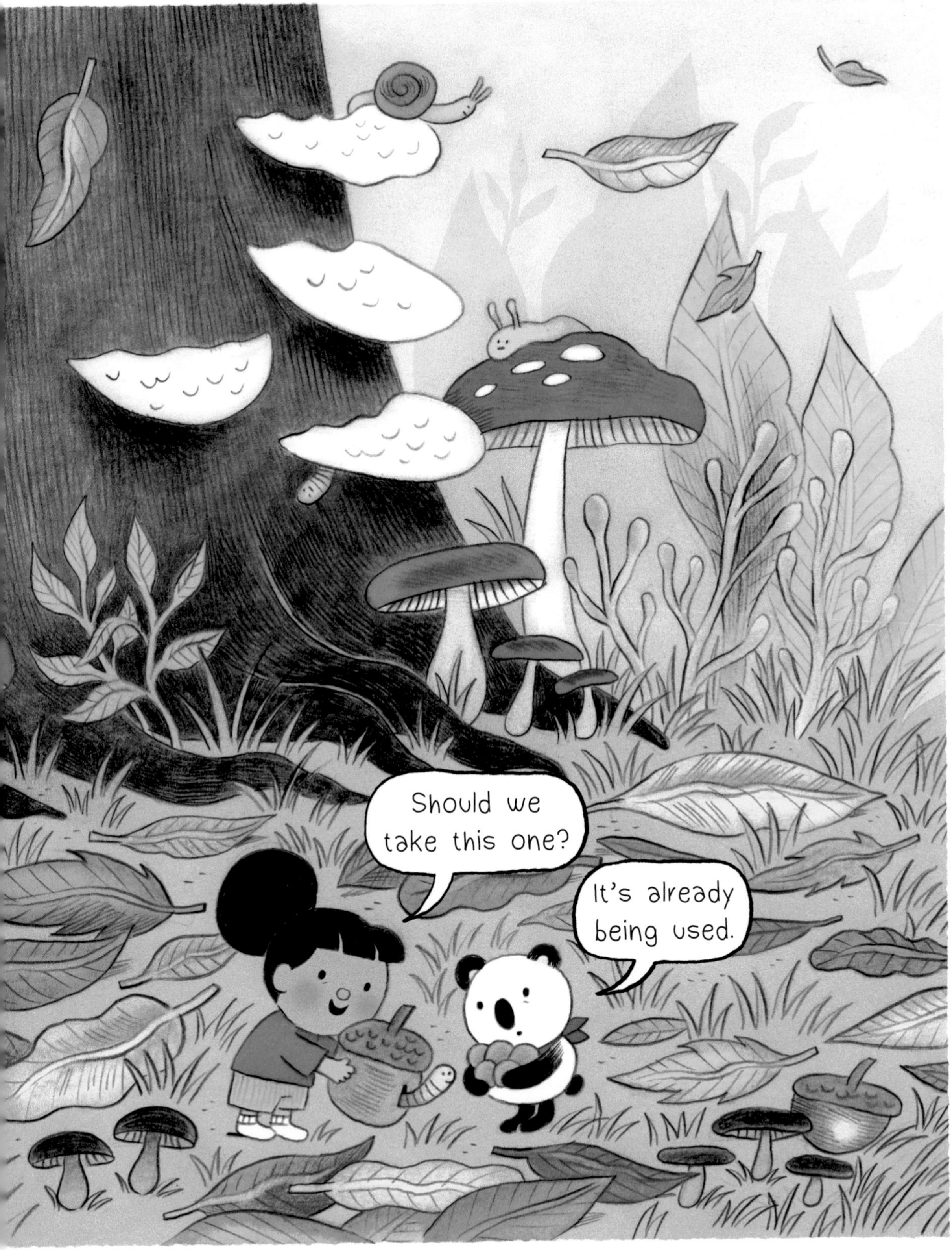
Should we take this one?
It's already being used.

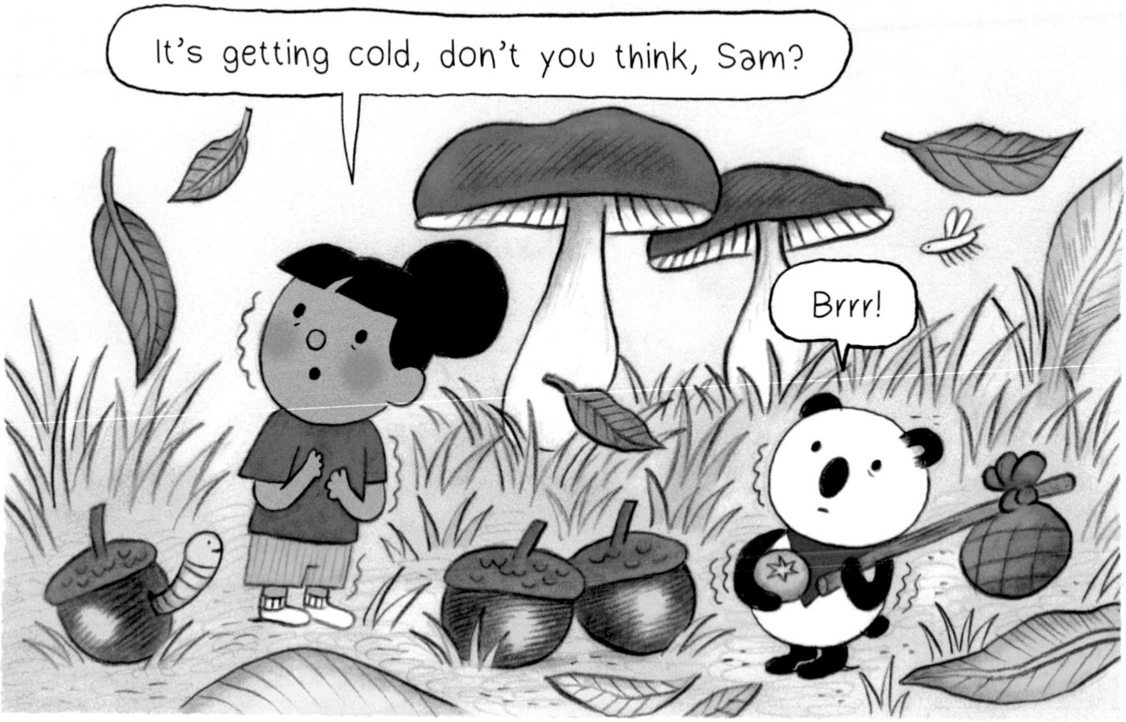
It's getting cold, don't you think, Sam?
Brrr!

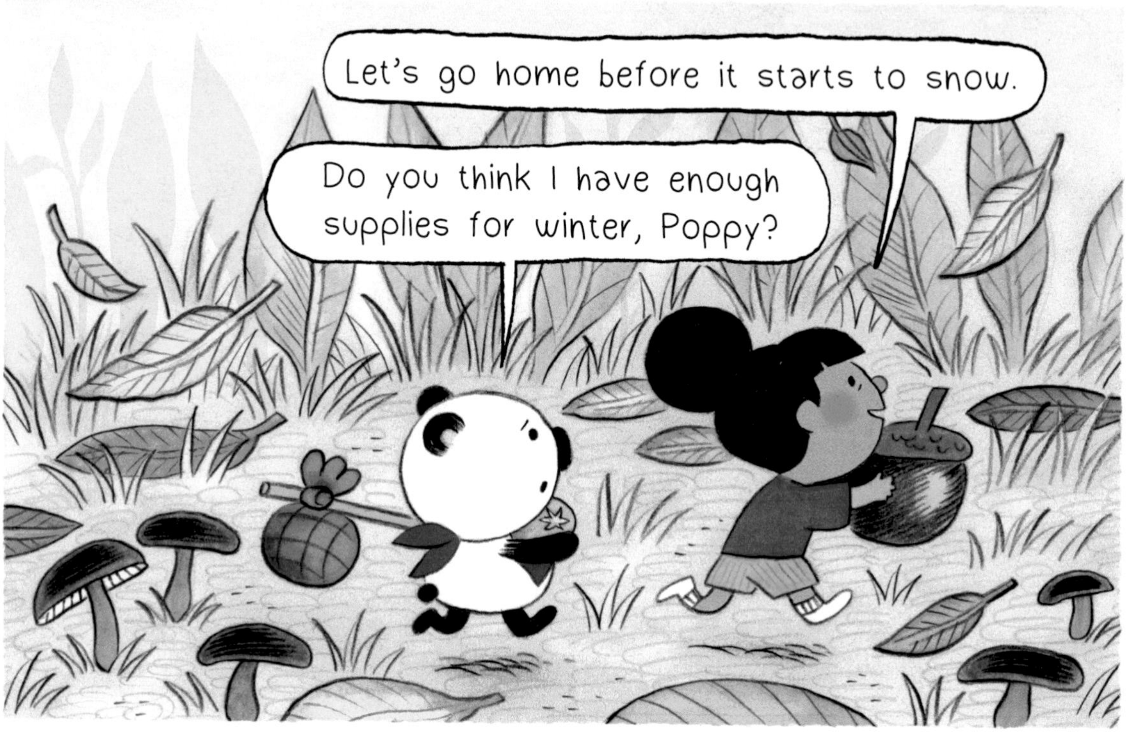
Let's go home before it starts to snow.
Do you think I have enough supplies for winter, Poppy?

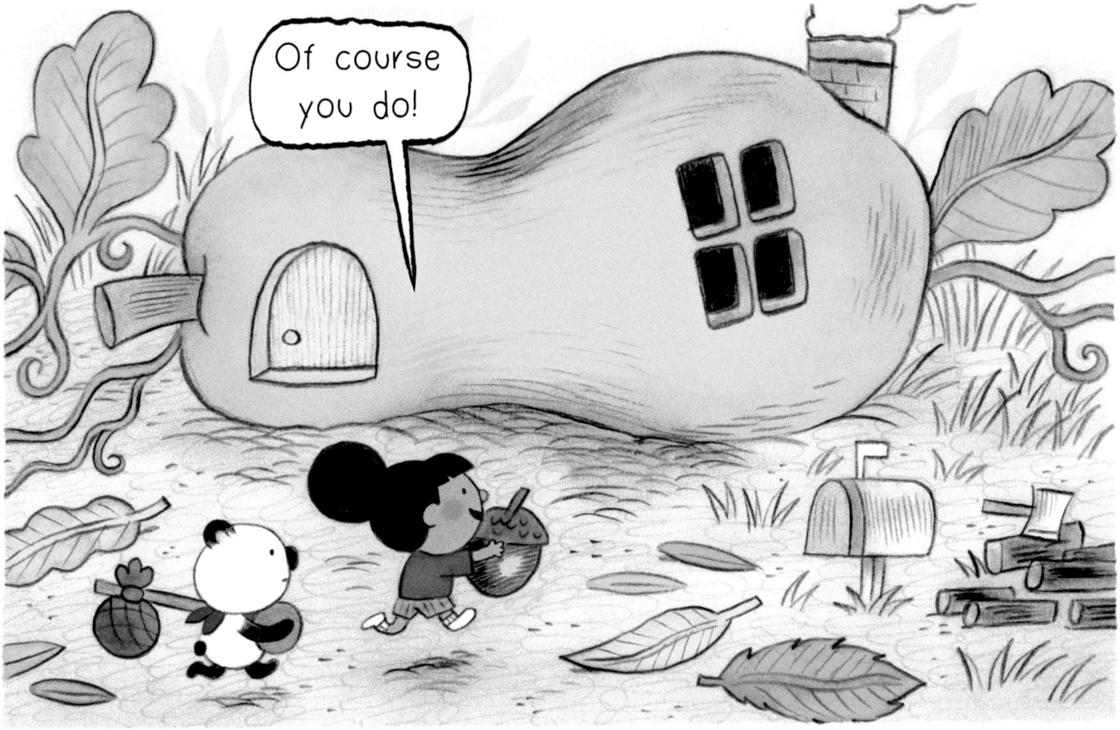
Of course you do!

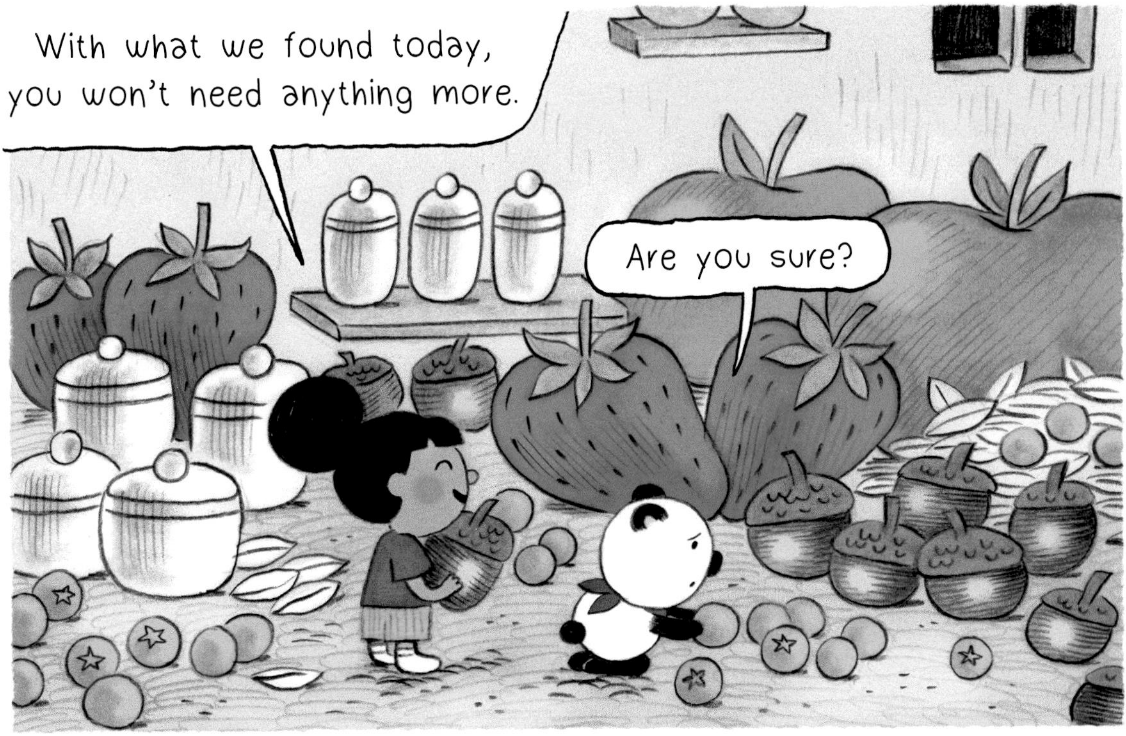
With what we found today, you won't need anything more.
Are you sure?

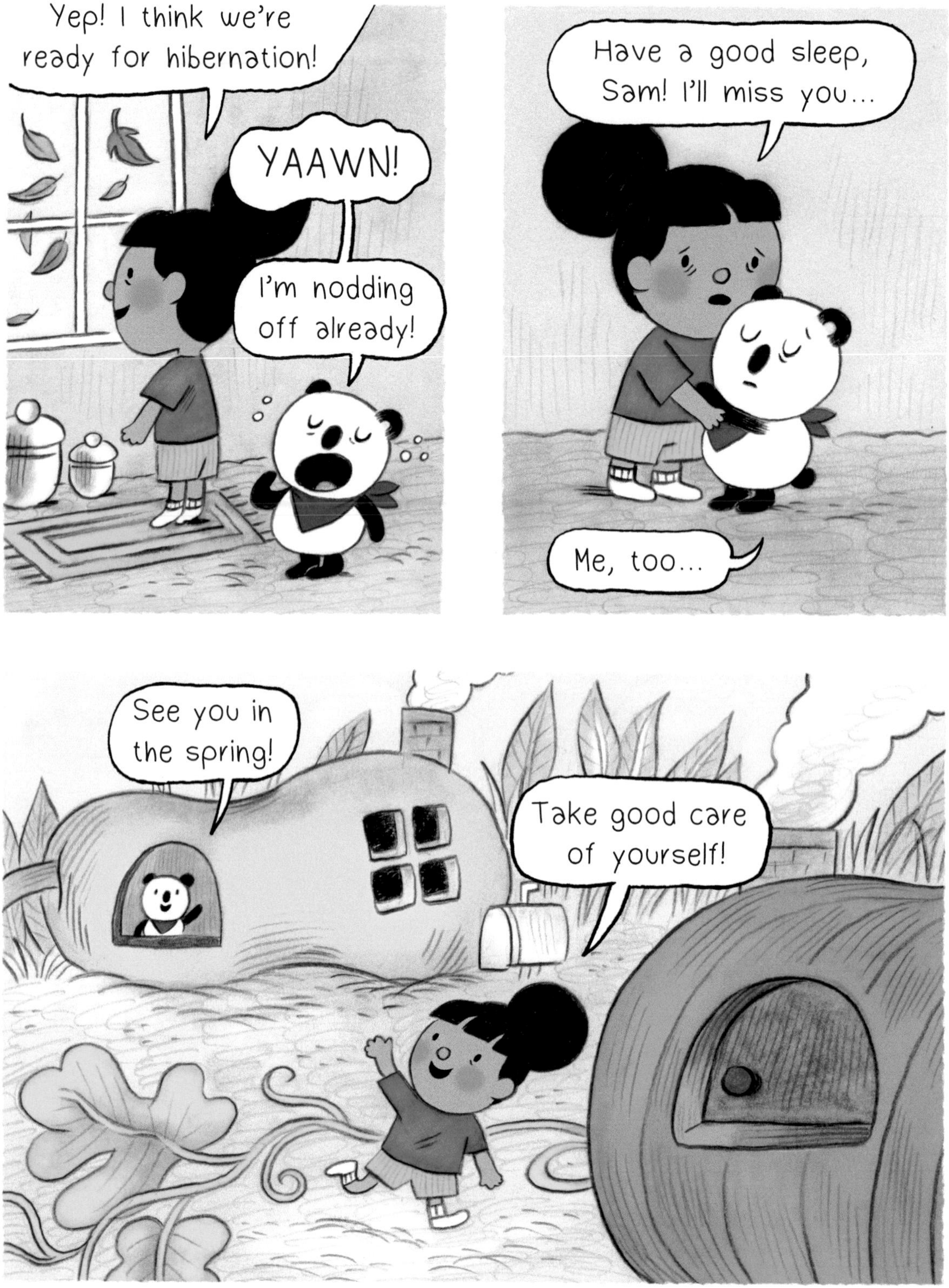
Yep! I think we're ready for hibernation!
YAAWN!
I'm nodding off already!
Have a good sleep, Sam! I'll miss you...
Me, too...
See you in the spring!
Take good care of yourself!

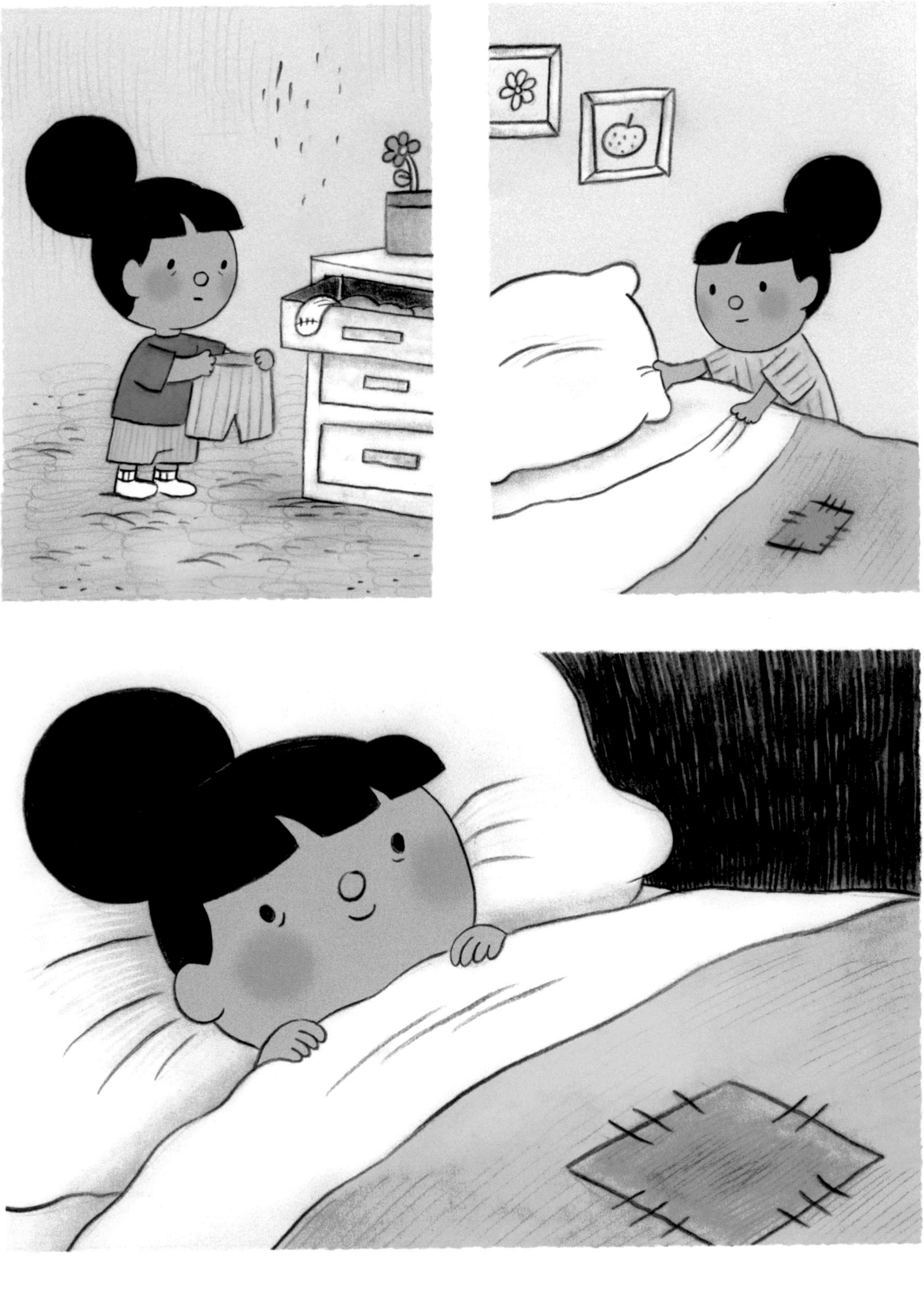

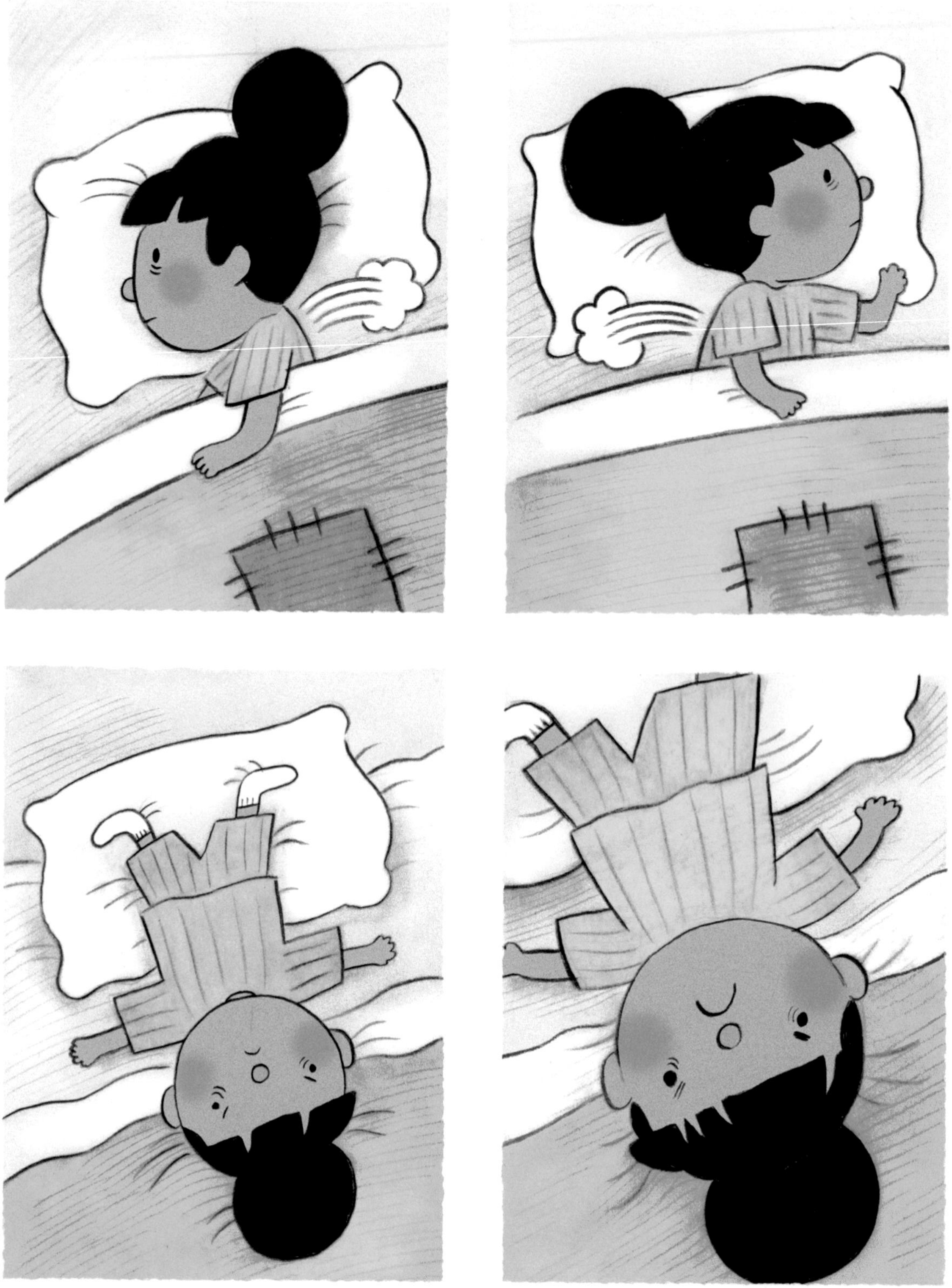

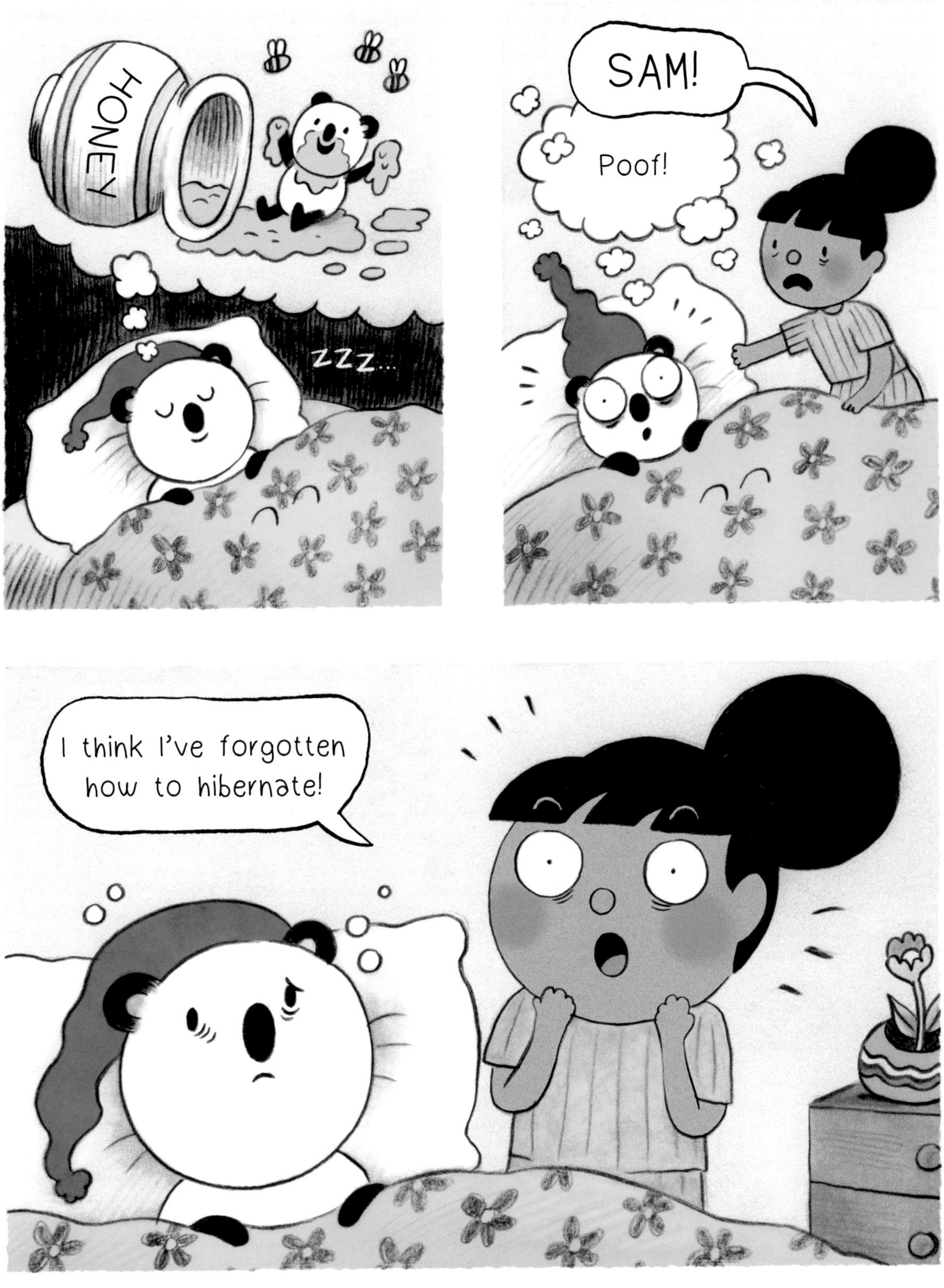
HONEY
ZZZ...
SAM!
Poof!
I think I've forgotten how to hibernate!

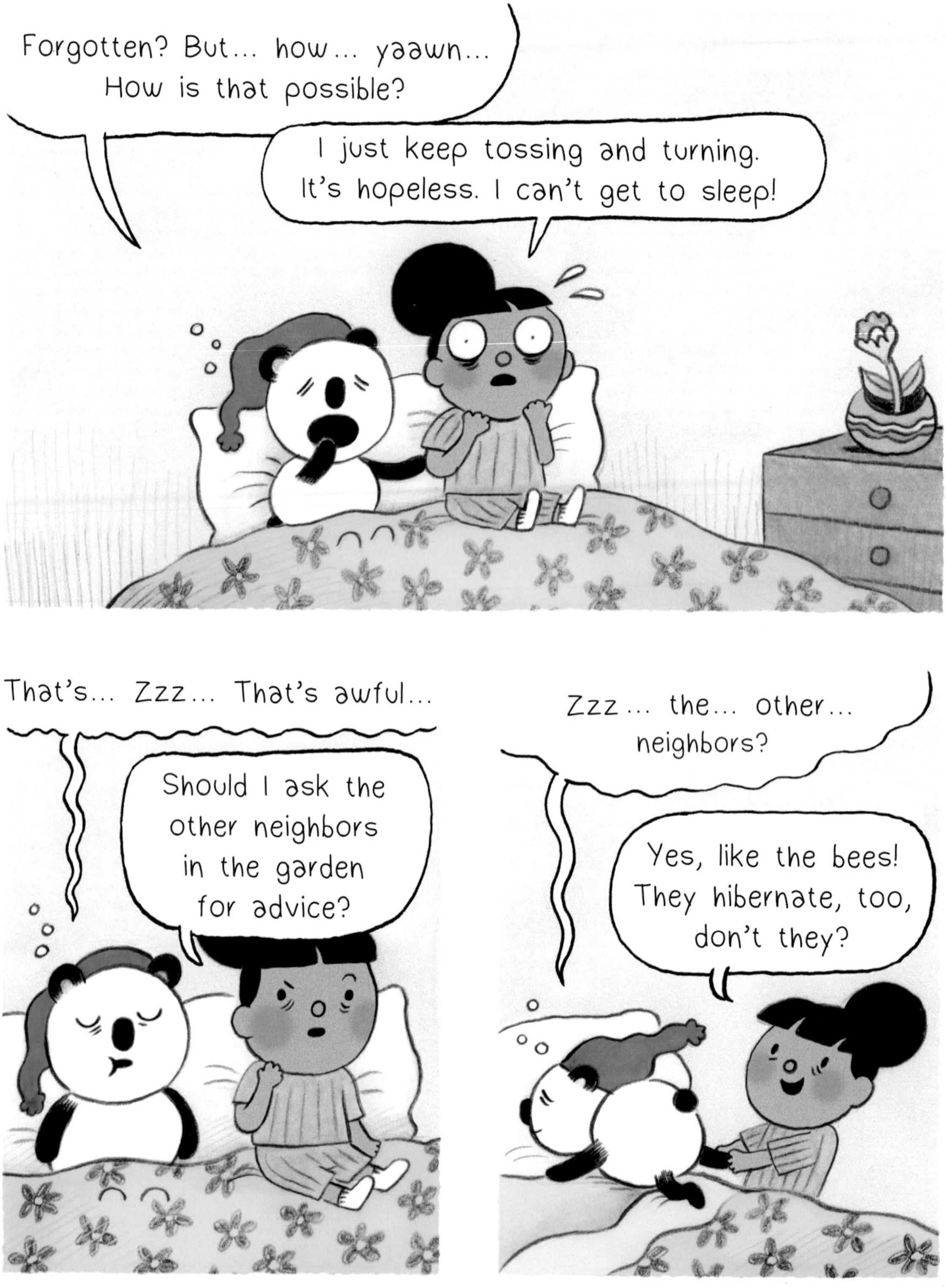
Forgotten? But... how... yaawn... How is that possible?
I just keep tossing and turning. It's hopeless. I can't get to sleep!
That's... Zzz... That's awful...
Should I ask the other neighbors in the garden for advice?
Zzz... the... other... neighbors?
Yes, like the bees! They hibernate, too, don't they?

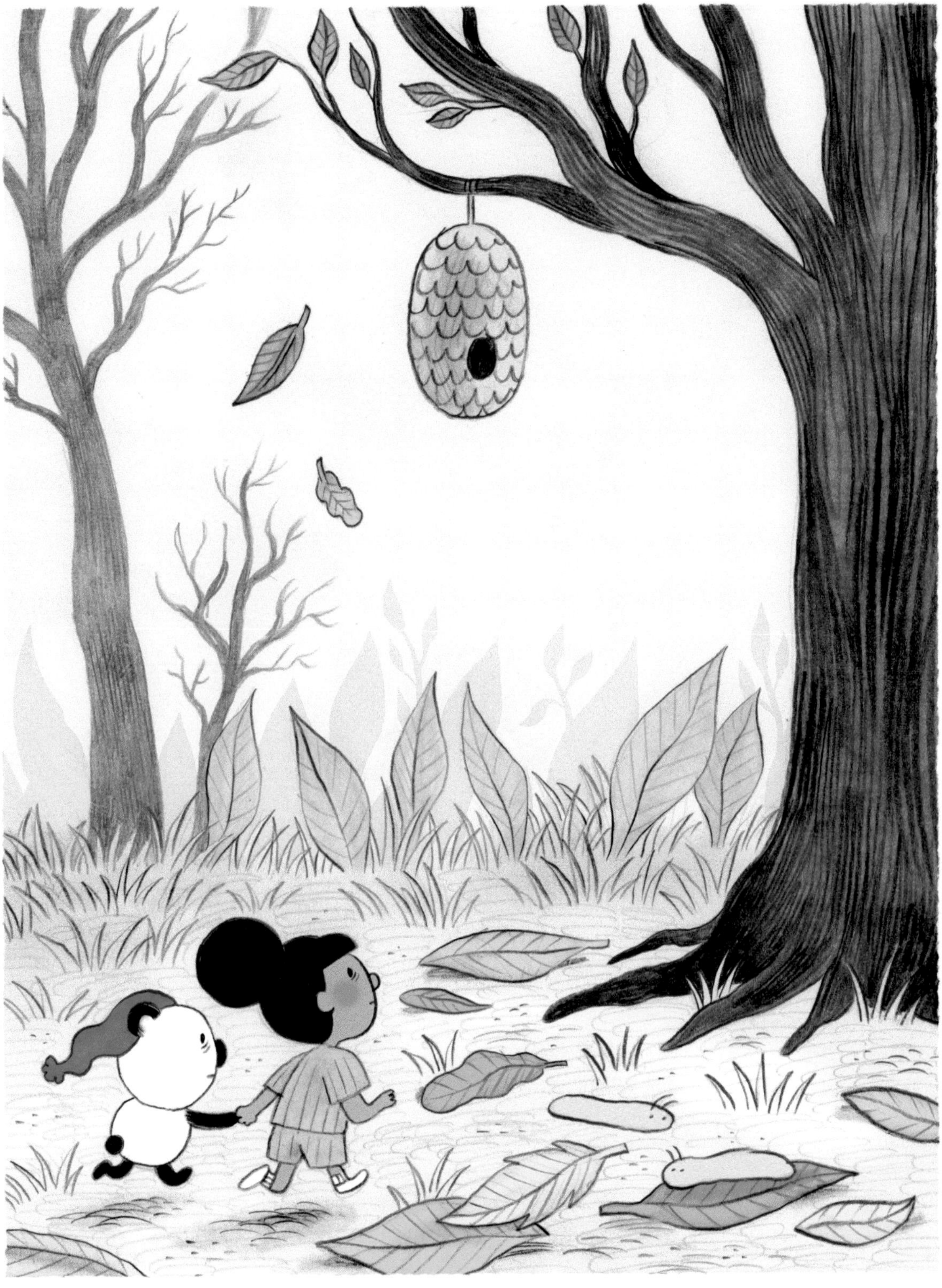

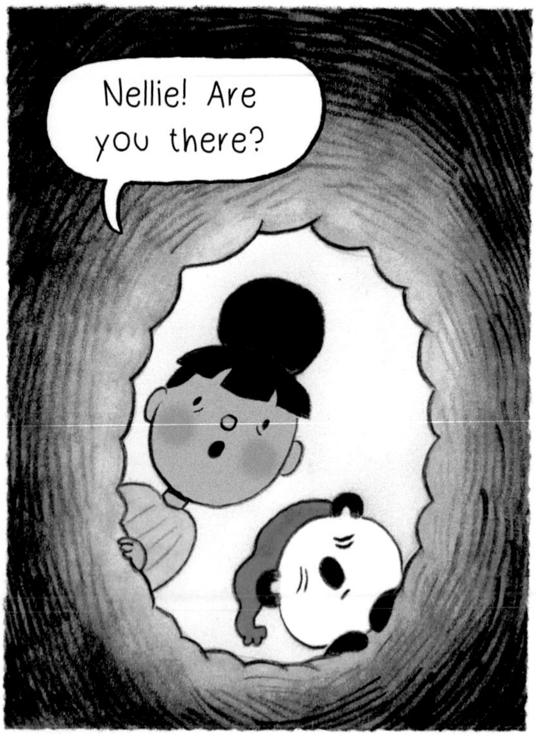
Nellie! Are you there?

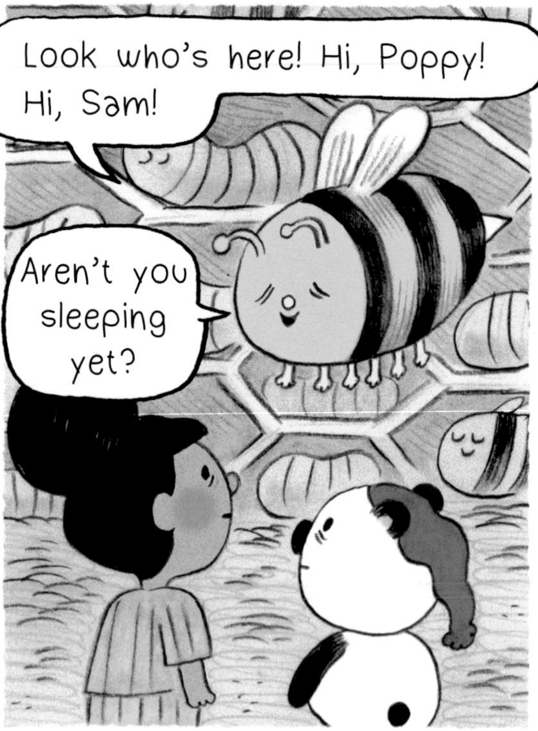
Look who's here! Hi, Poppy! Hi, Sam!
Aren't you sleeping yet?

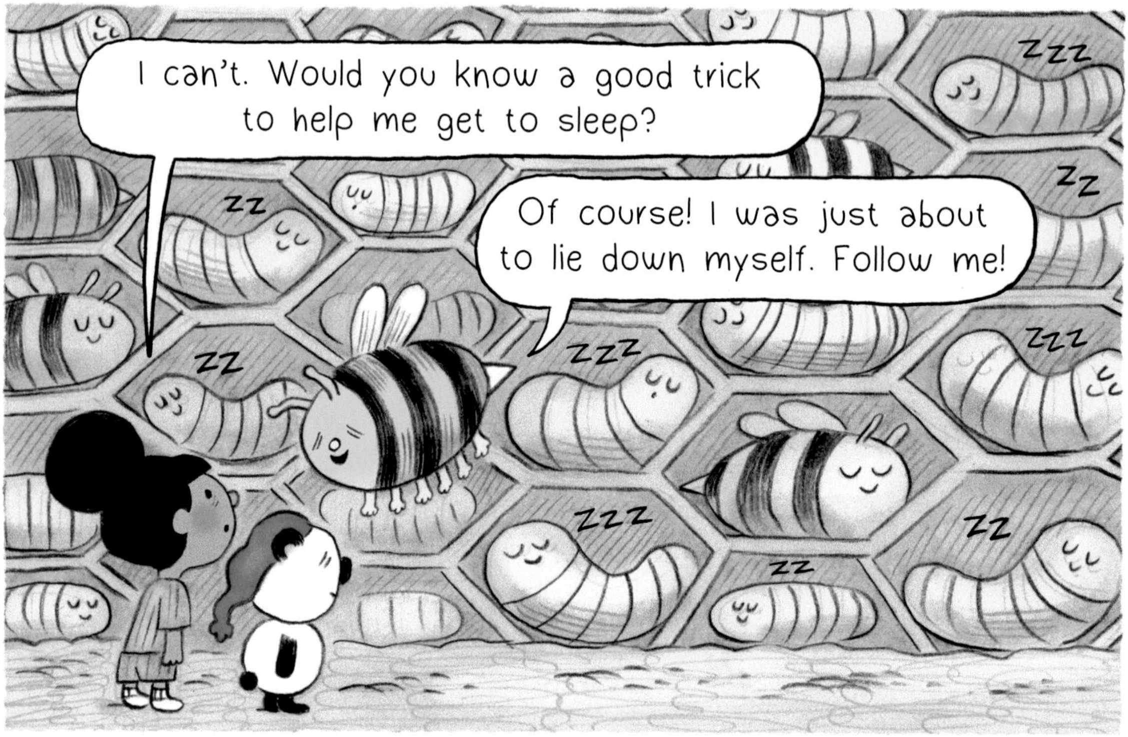
I can't. Would you know a good trick to help me get to sleep?
Of course! I was just about to lie down myself. Follow me!
ZZZ
ZZ
ZZ
ZZ
ZZZ
ZZZ
ZZZ
ZZ
ZZ

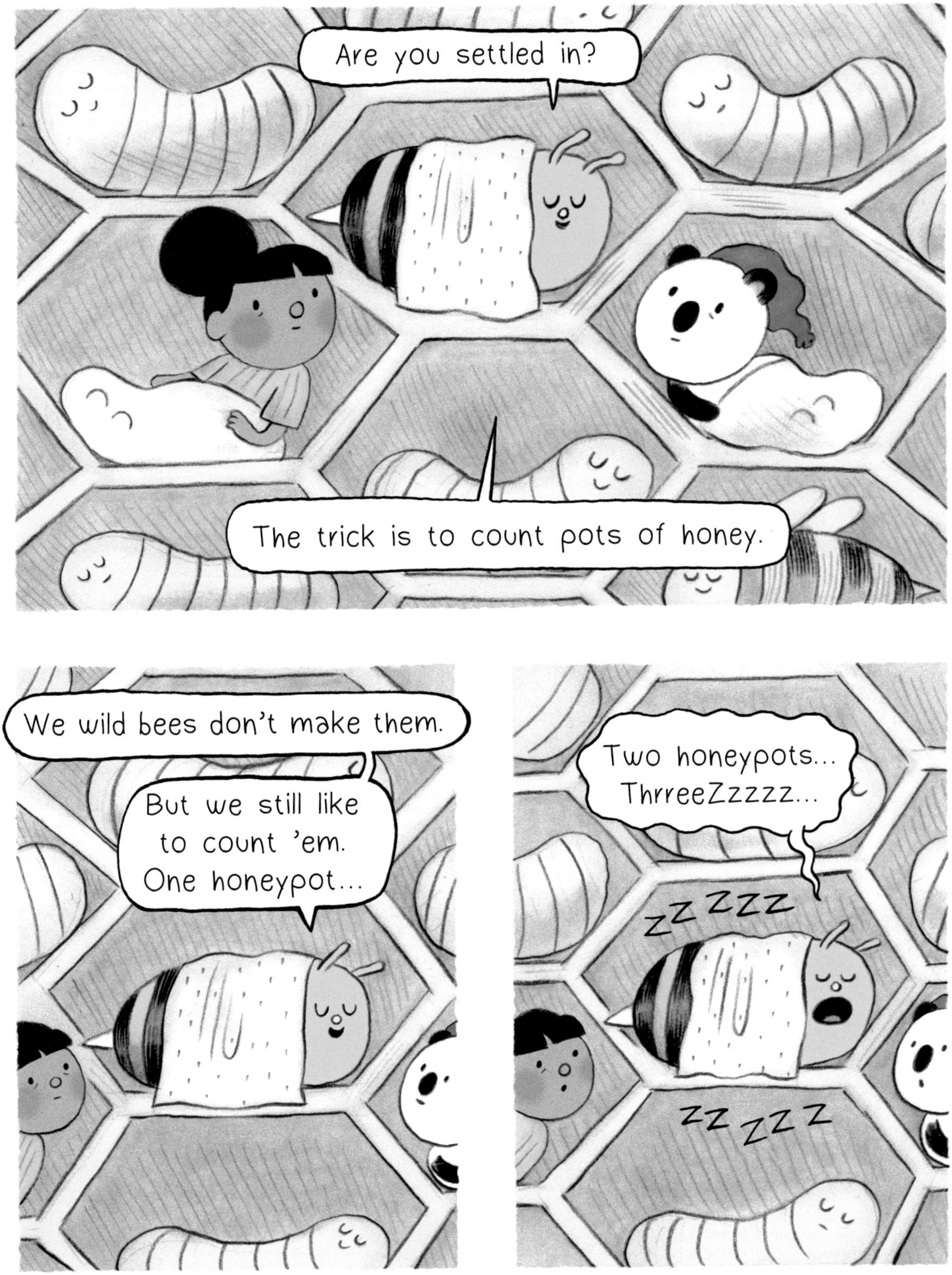
Are you settled in?
The trick is to count pots of honey.
We wild bees don't make them.
But we still like to count 'em. One honeypot...
Two honeypots... ThrreeZzzzz...
ZZZZZ
ZZZZZ

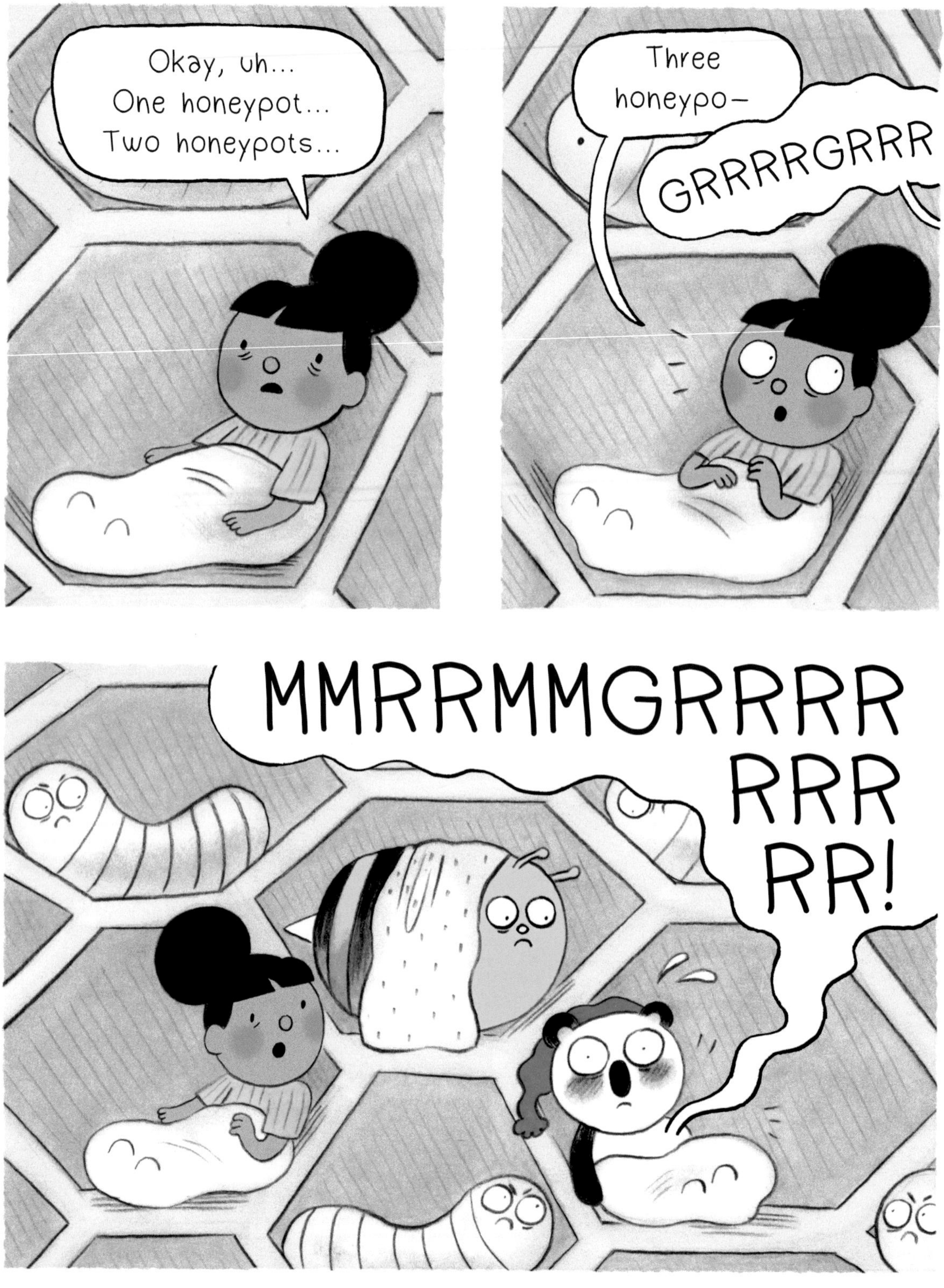
Okay, uh... One honeypot... Two honeypots...
Three honeypo–
GRRRRGRRR
MMRRMMGRRRR RRR RR!

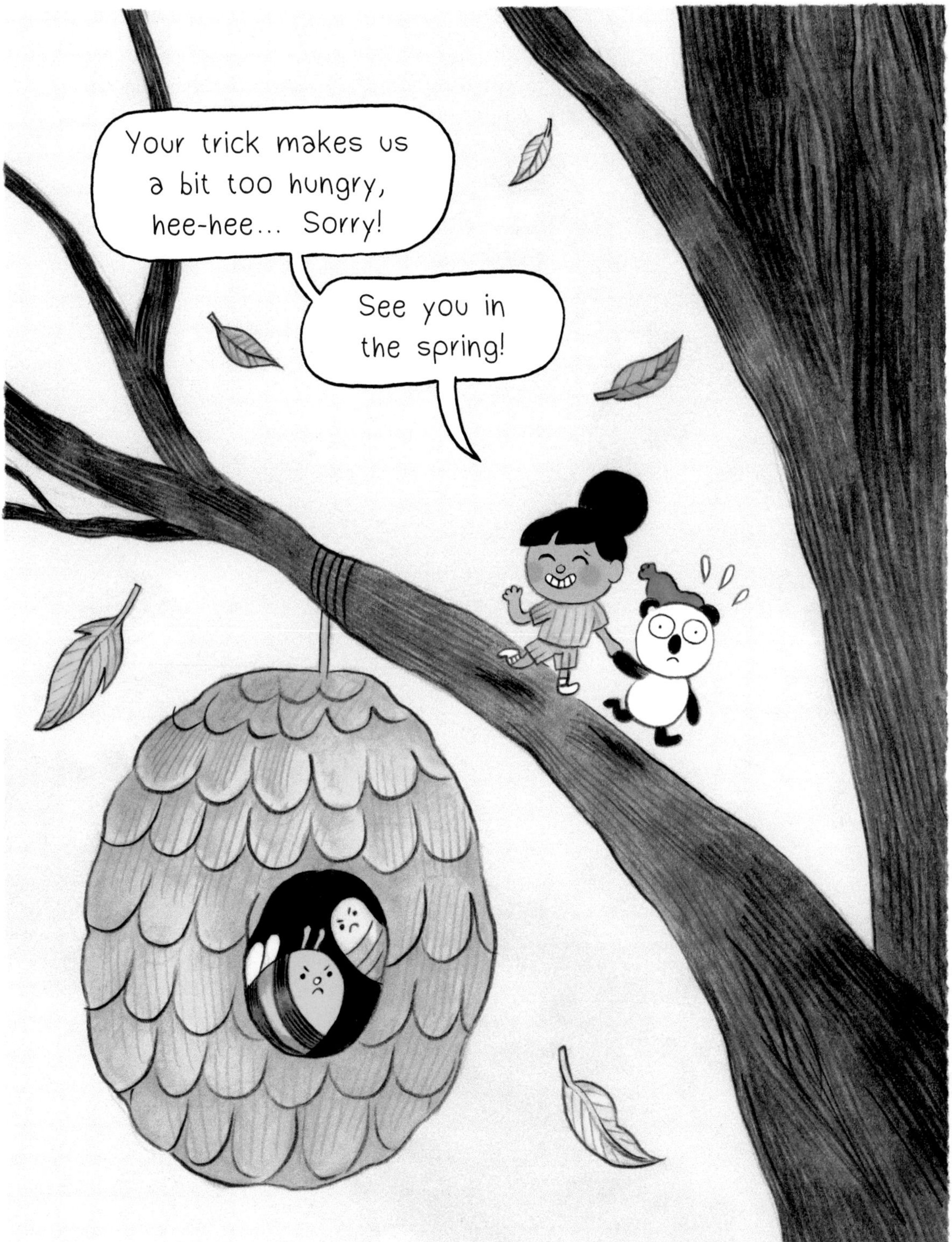
Your trick makes us a bit too hungry, hee-hee... Sorry!
See you in the spring!

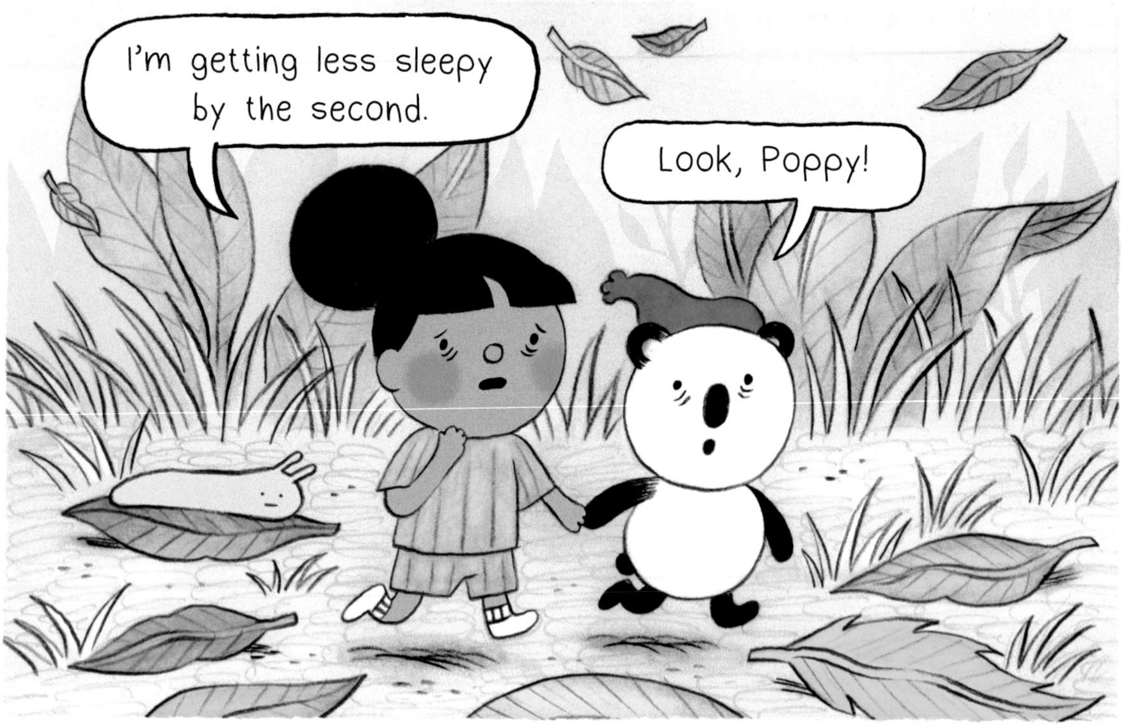
I'm getting less sleepy by the second.
Look, Poppy!

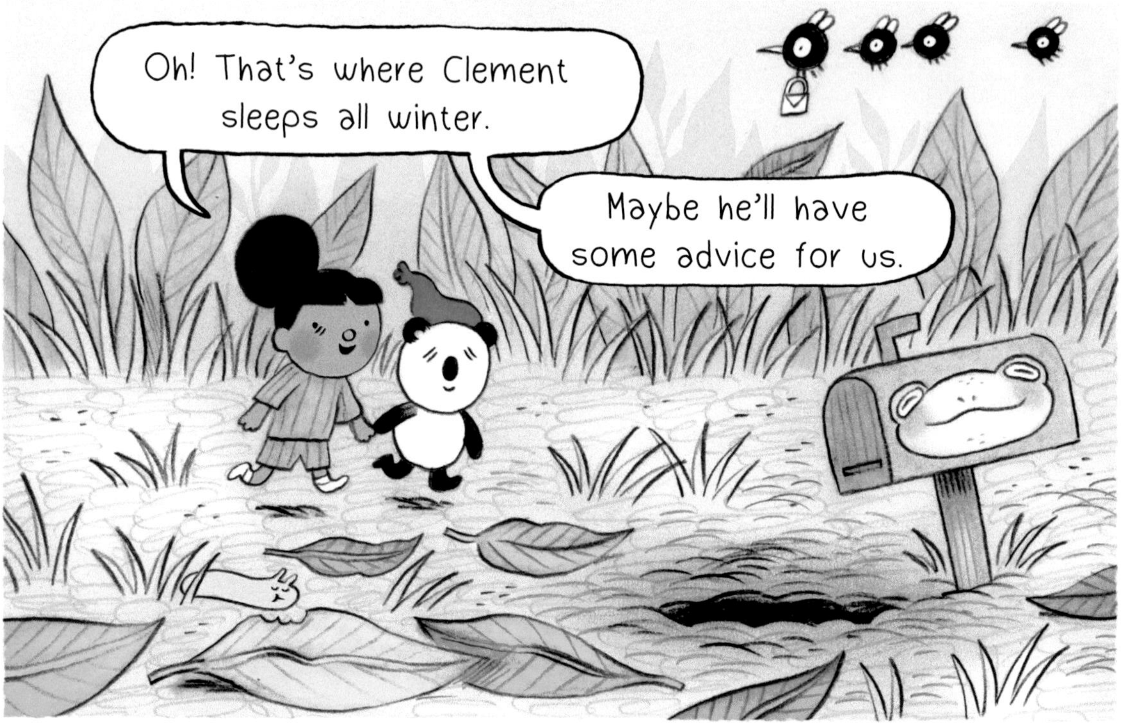
Oh! That's where Clement sleeps all winter.
Maybe he'll have some advice for us.

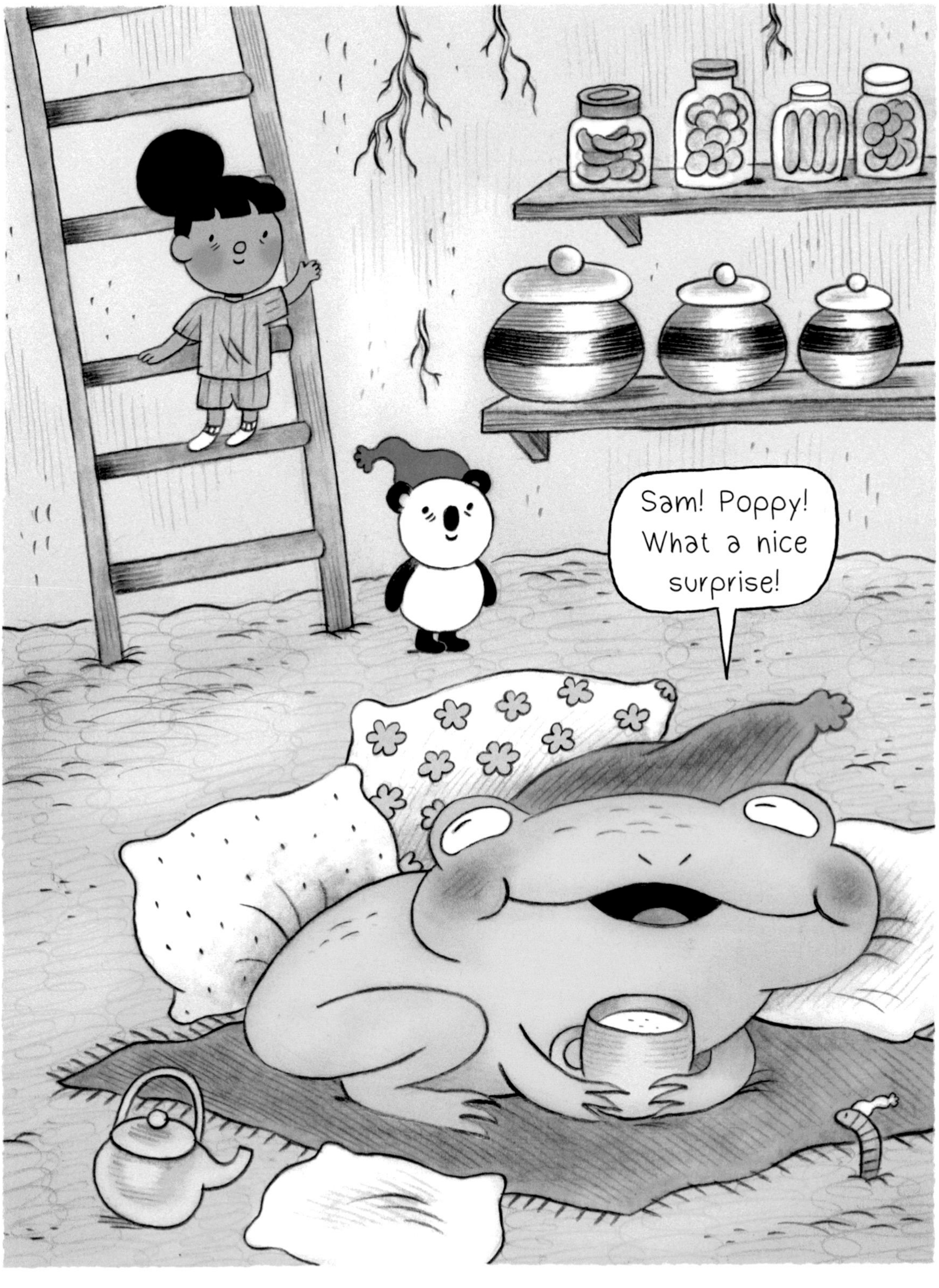
Sam! Poppy! What a nice surprise!

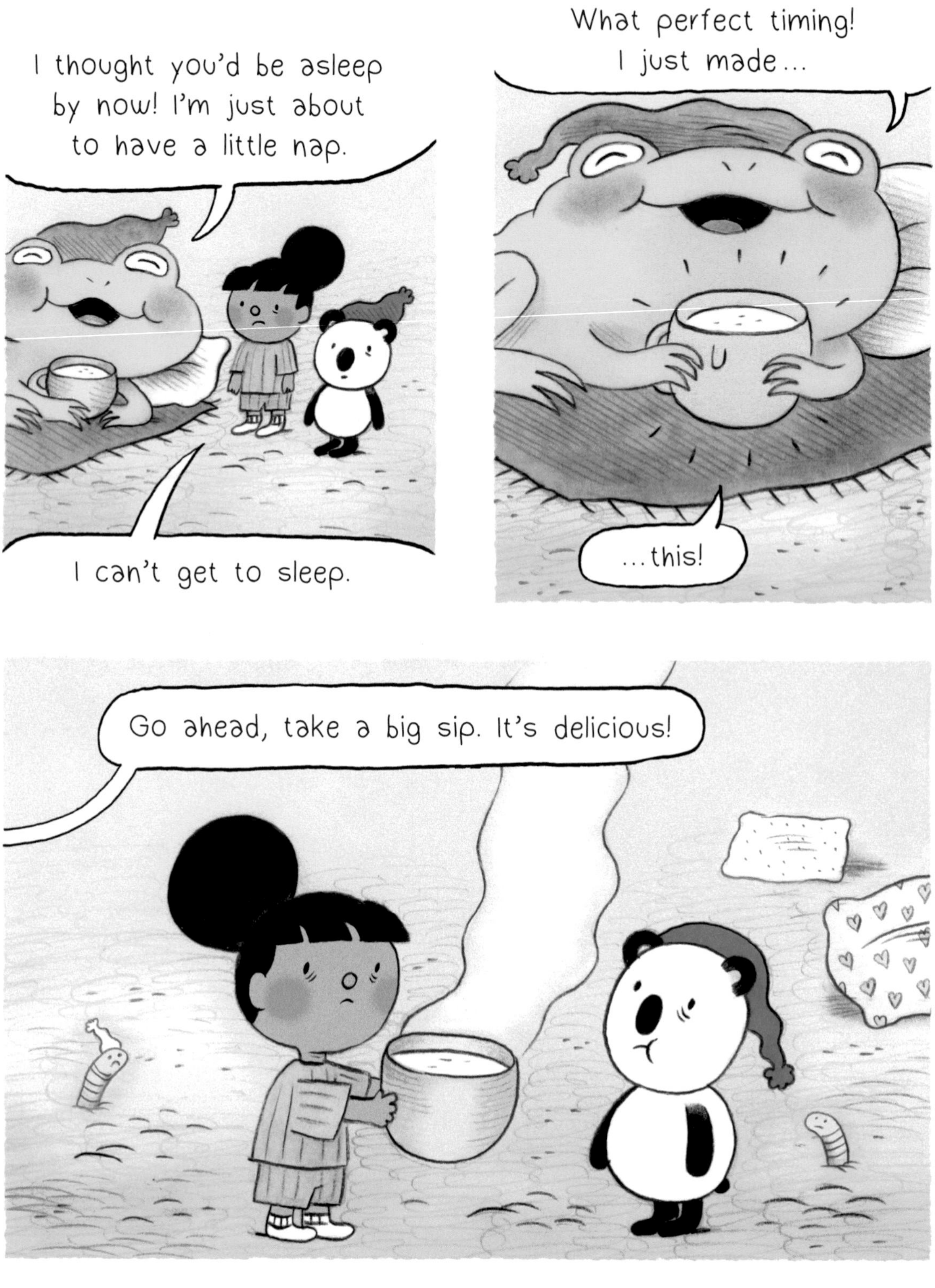
I thought you'd be asleep by now! I'm just about to have a little nap.
I can't get to sleep.
What perfect timing! I just made...
...this!
Go ahead, take a big sip. It's delicious!

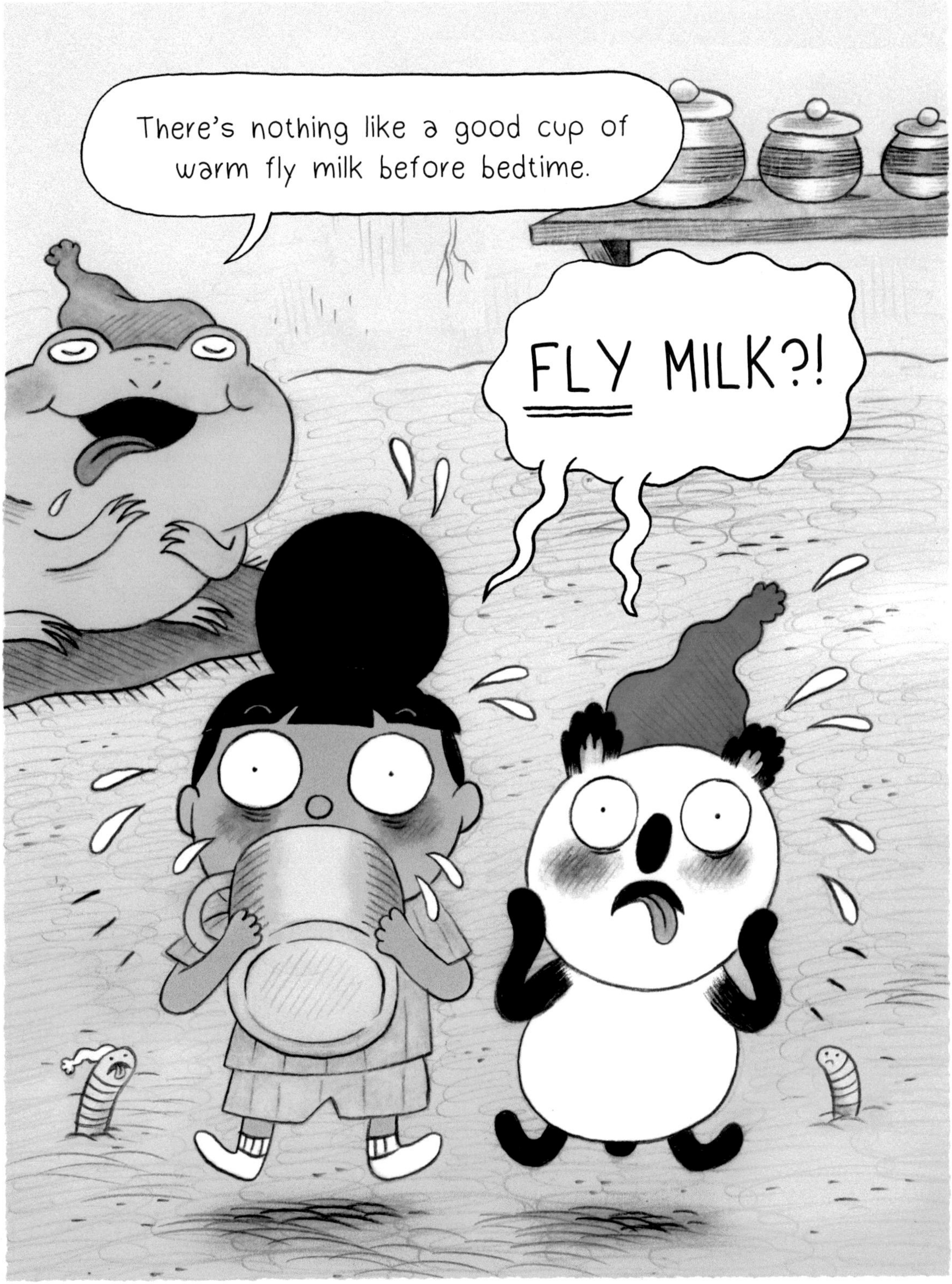
There's nothing like a good cup of warm fly milk before bedtime.
FLY MILK?!

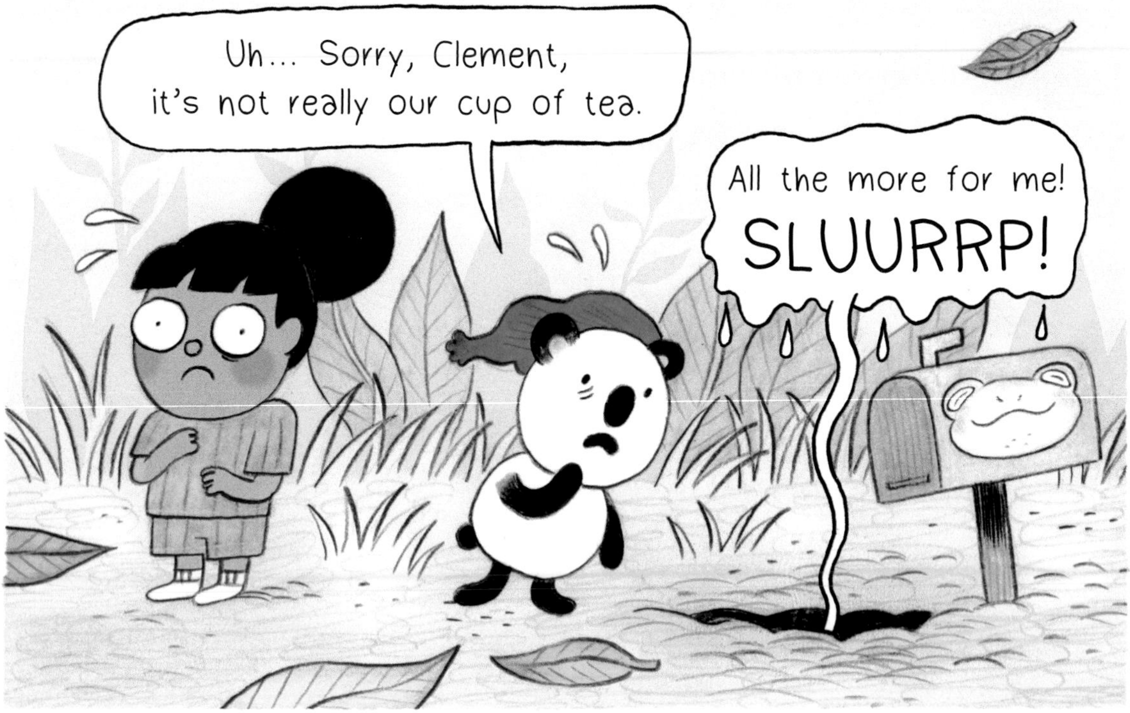
Uh... Sorry, Clement, it's not really our cup of tea.
All the more for me!
SLUURRP!

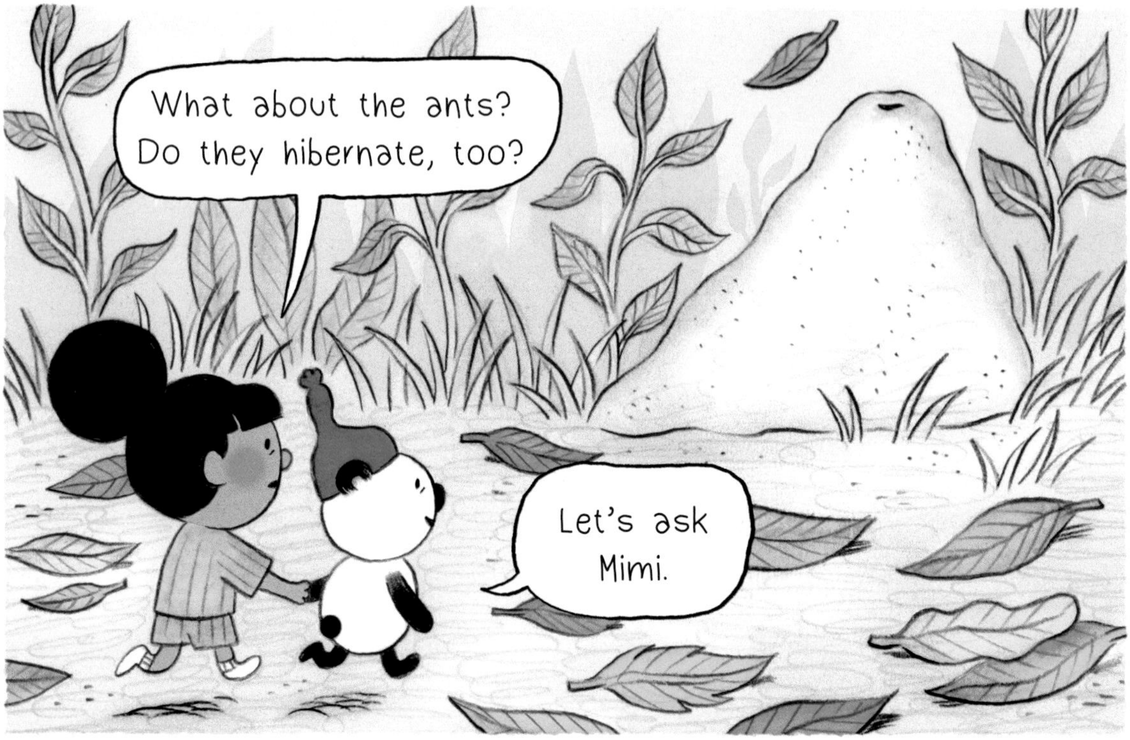
What about the ants? Do they hibernate, too?
Let's ask Mimi.

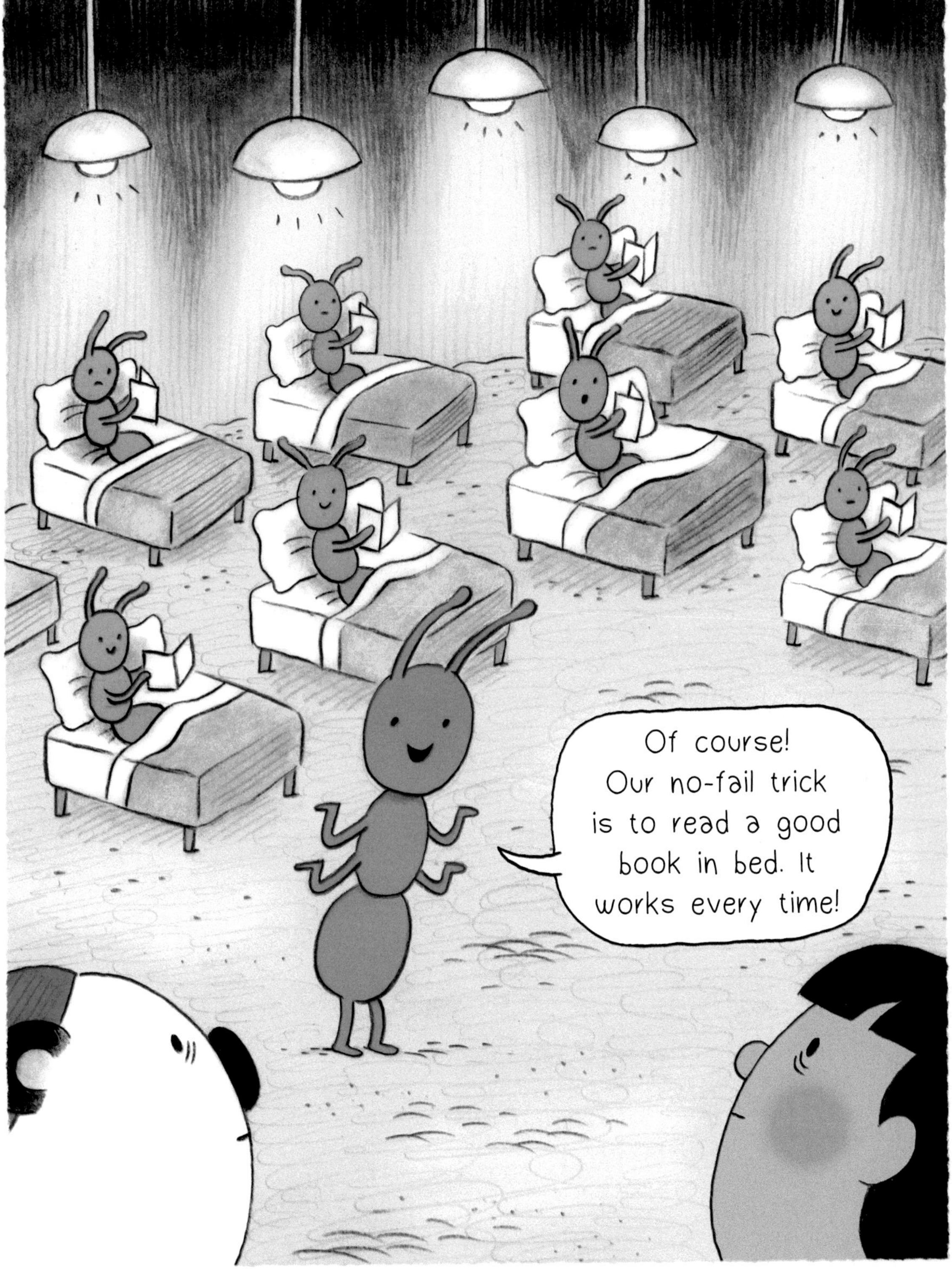
Of course! Our no-fail trick is to read a good book in bed. It works every time!

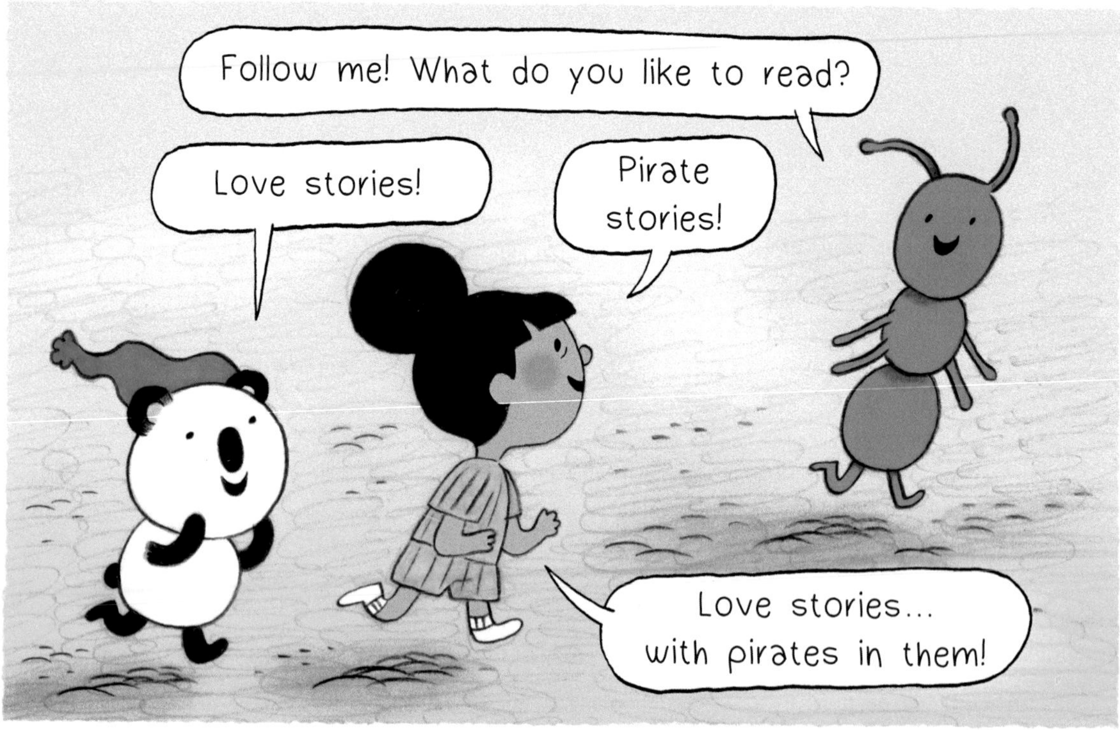
Follow me! What do you like to read?
Love stories!
Pirate stories!
Love stories... with pirates in them!

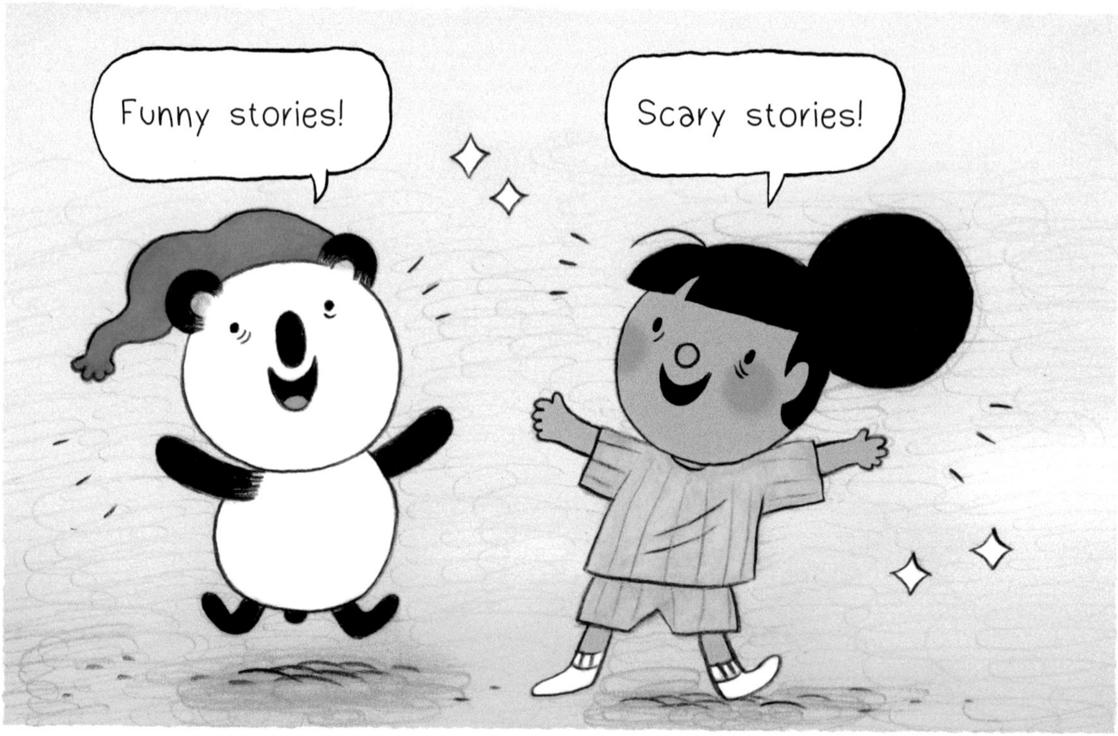
Funny stories!
Scary stories!

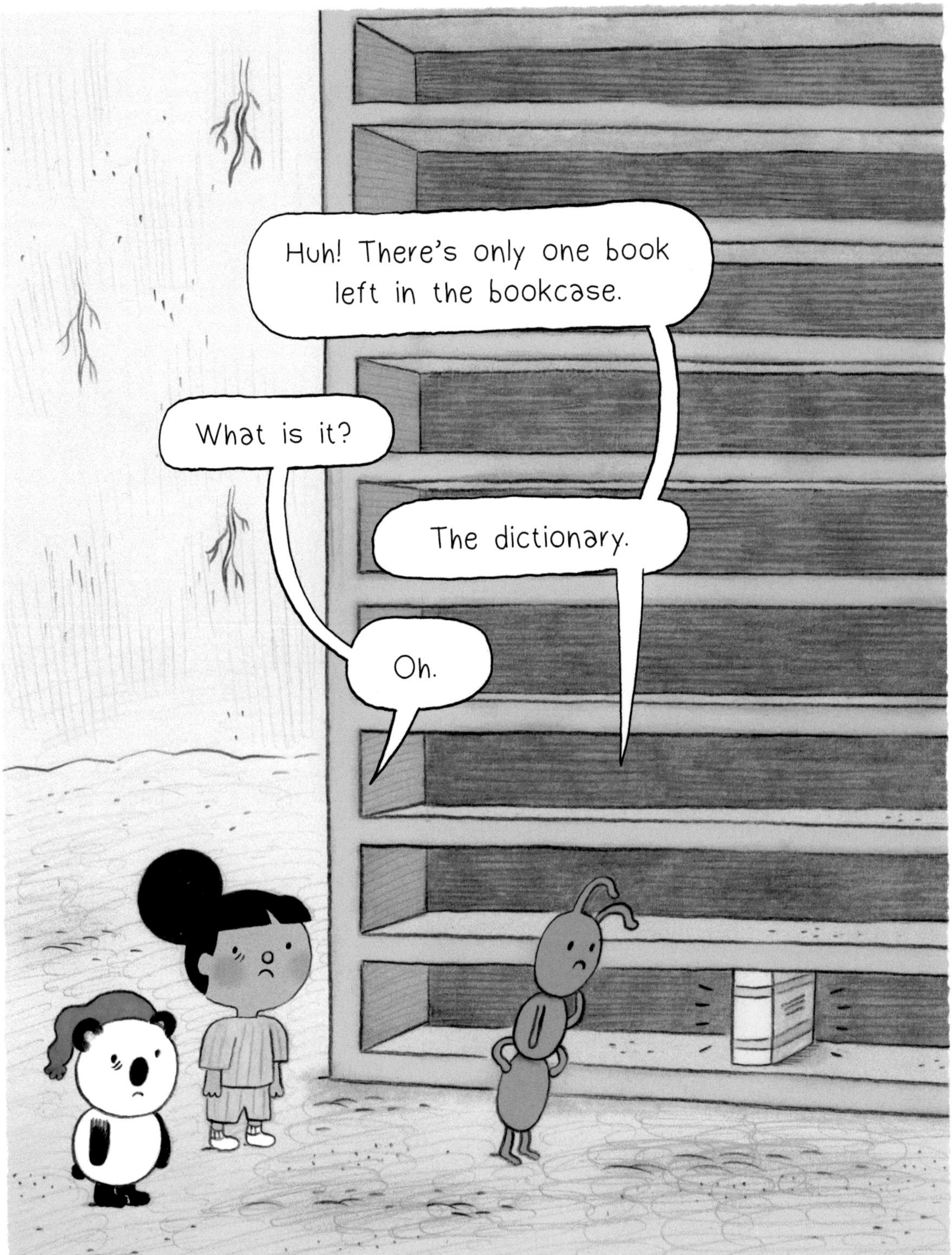
Huh! There's only one book left in the bookcase.
What is it?
The dictionary.
Oh.

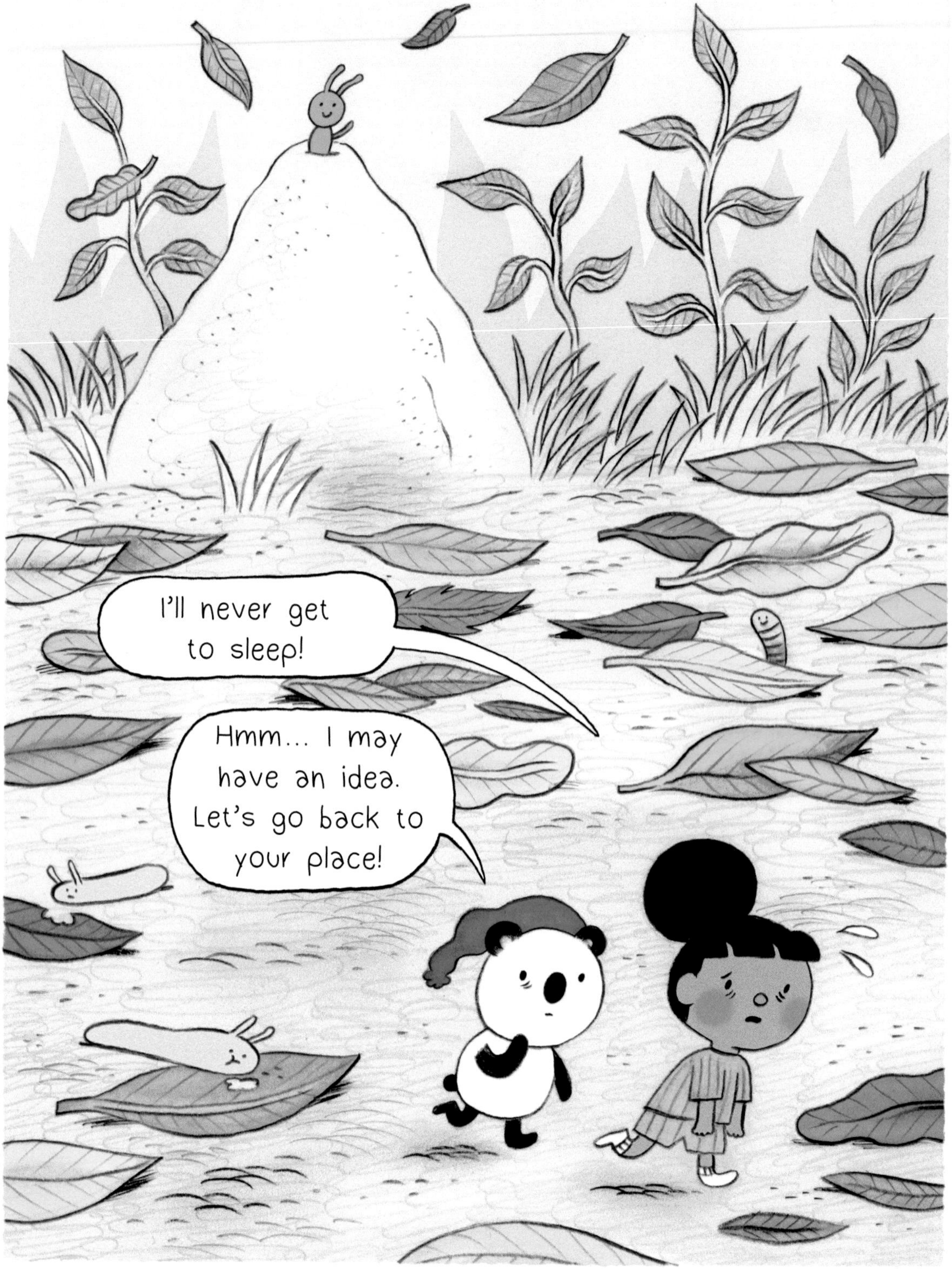
I'll never get to sleep!
Hmm... I may have an idea. Let's go back to your place!

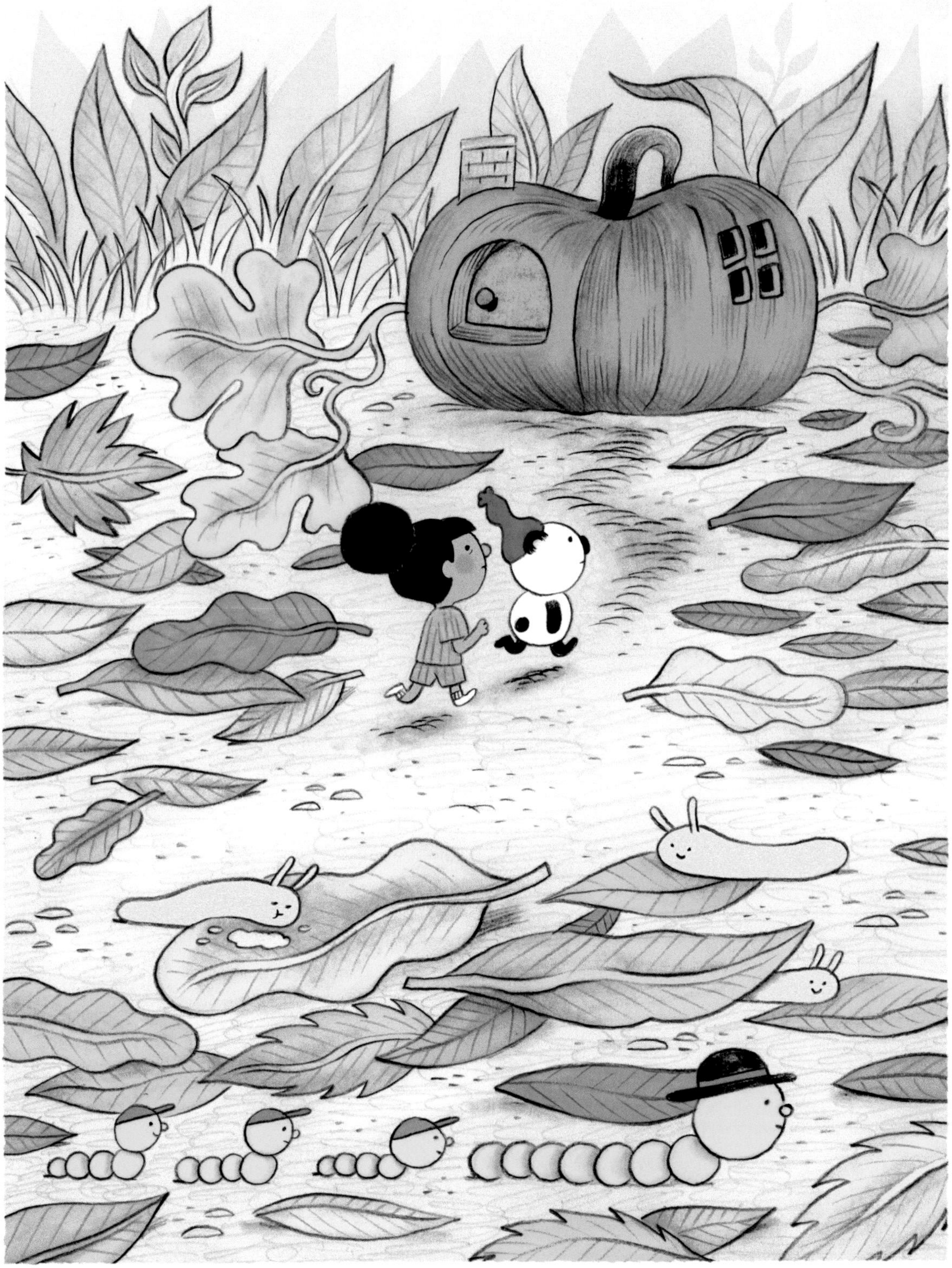

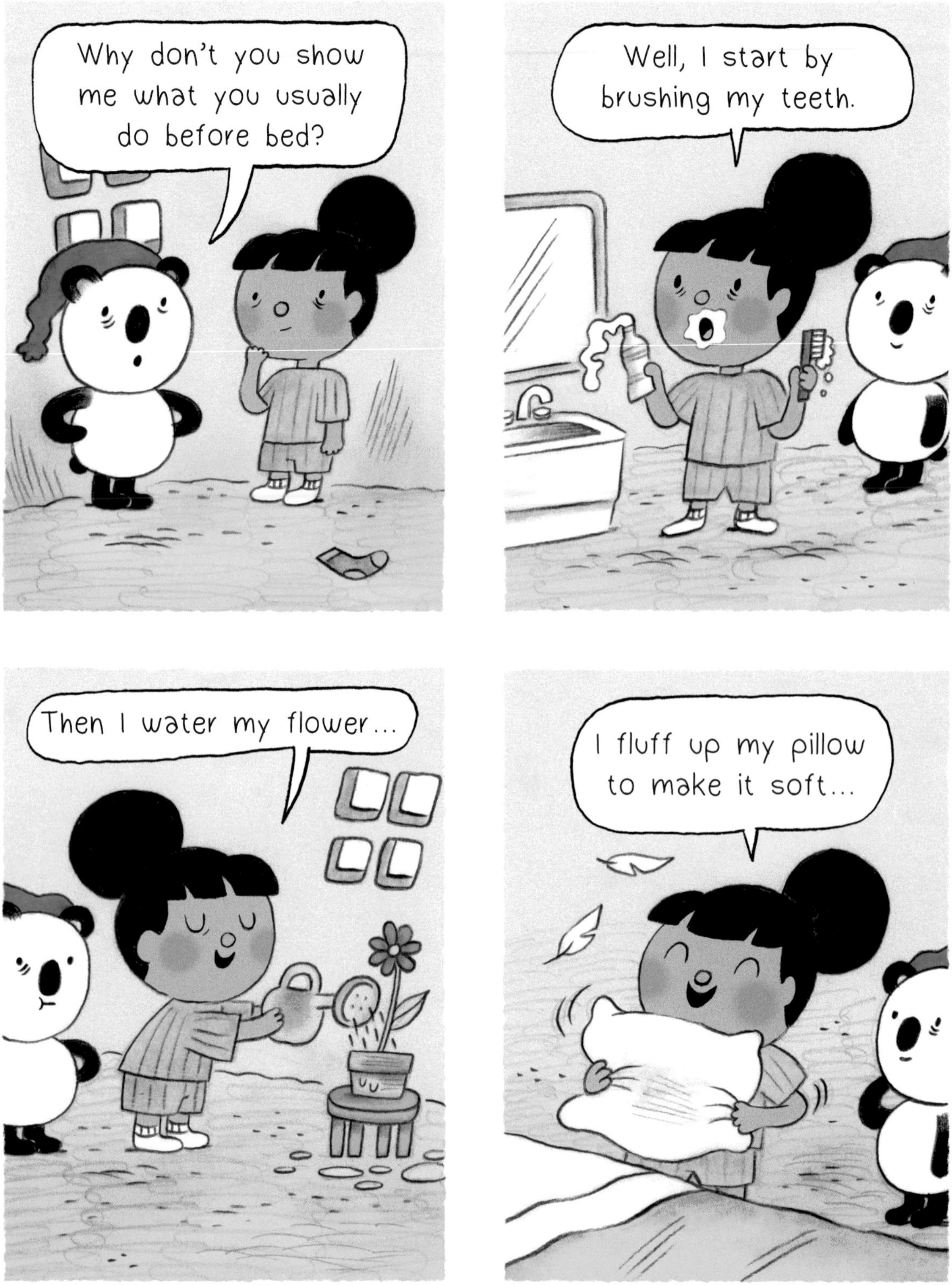
Why don't you show me what you usually do before bed?
Well, I start by brushing my teeth.
Then I water my flower...
I fluff up my pillow to make it soft...

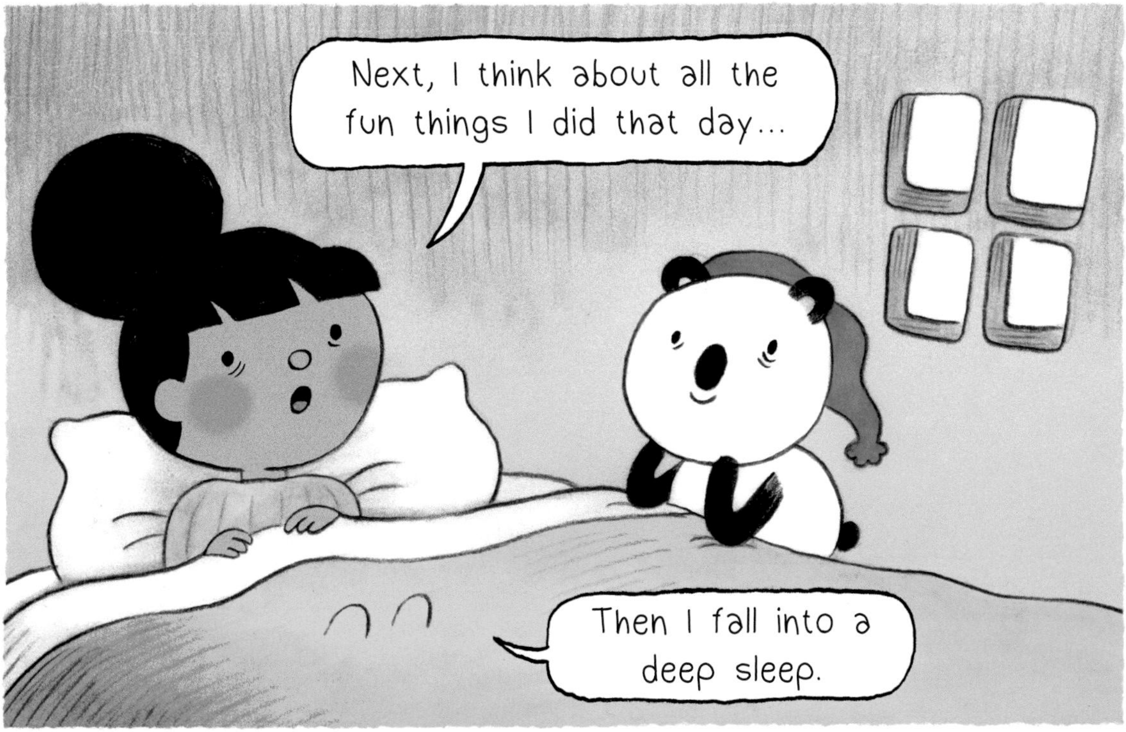
Next, I think about all the fun things I did that day...
Then I fall into a deep sleep.

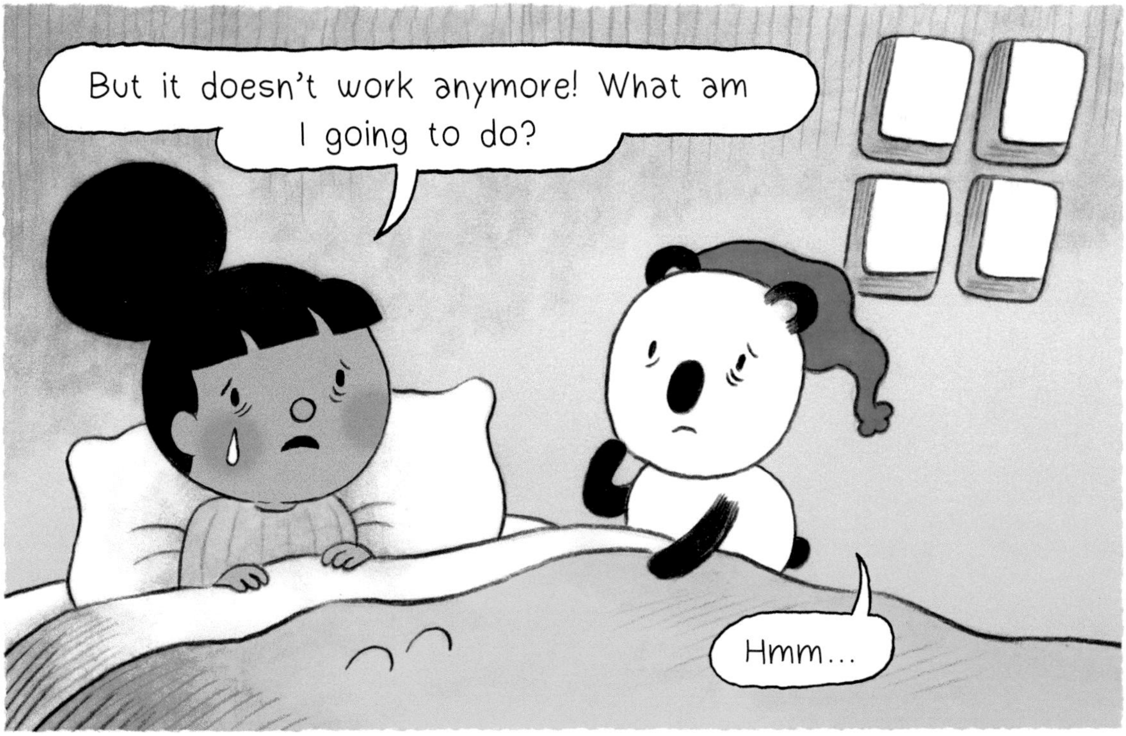
But it doesn't work anymore! What am I going to do?
Hmm...

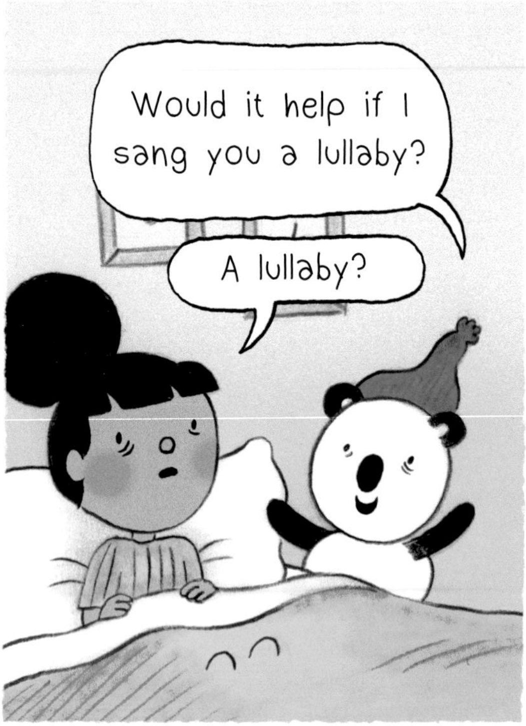
Would it help if I sang you a lullaby?
A lullaby?

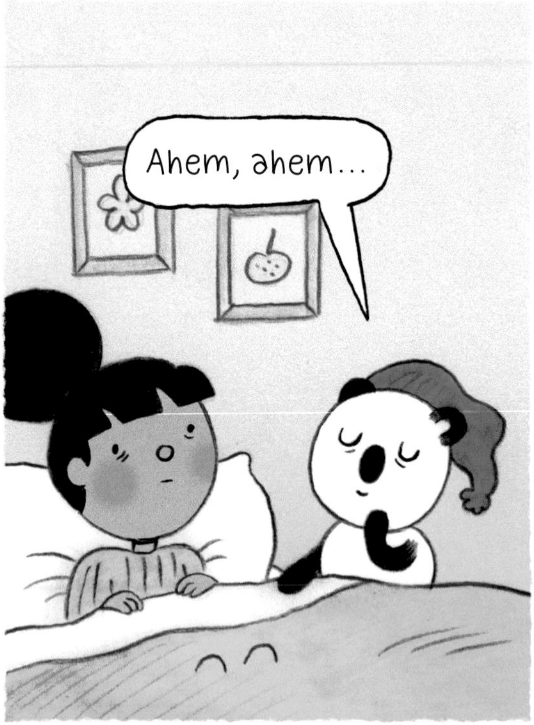
Ahem, ahem...

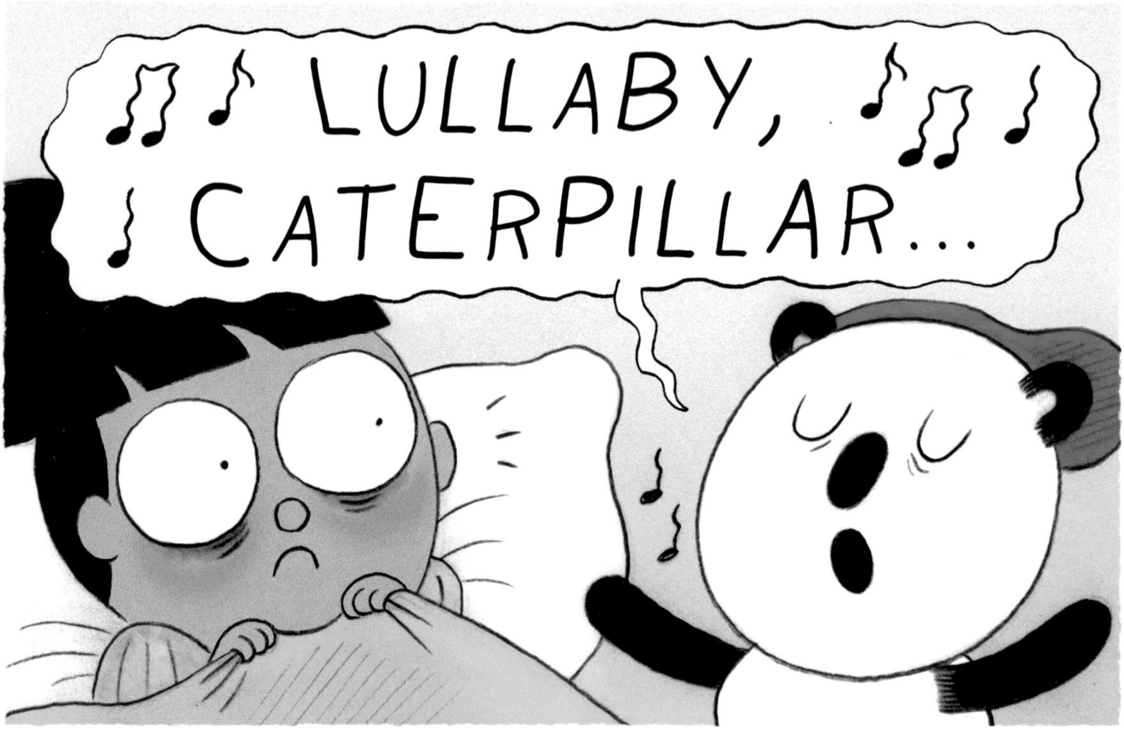
LULLABY, CATERPILLAR...

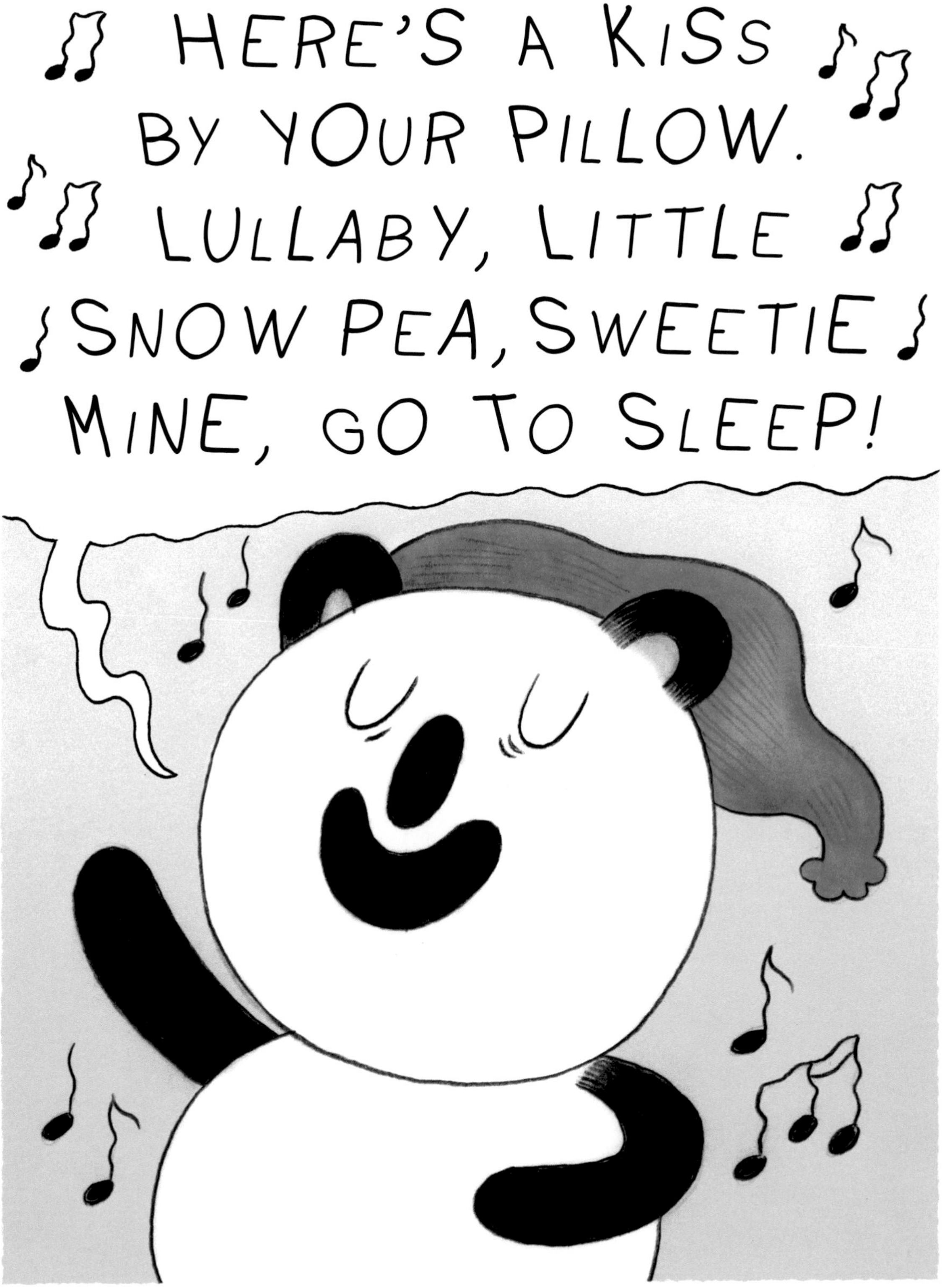
HERE'S A KISS BY YOUR PILLOW. LULLABY, LITTLE SNOW PEA, SWEETIE MINE, GO TO SLEEP!

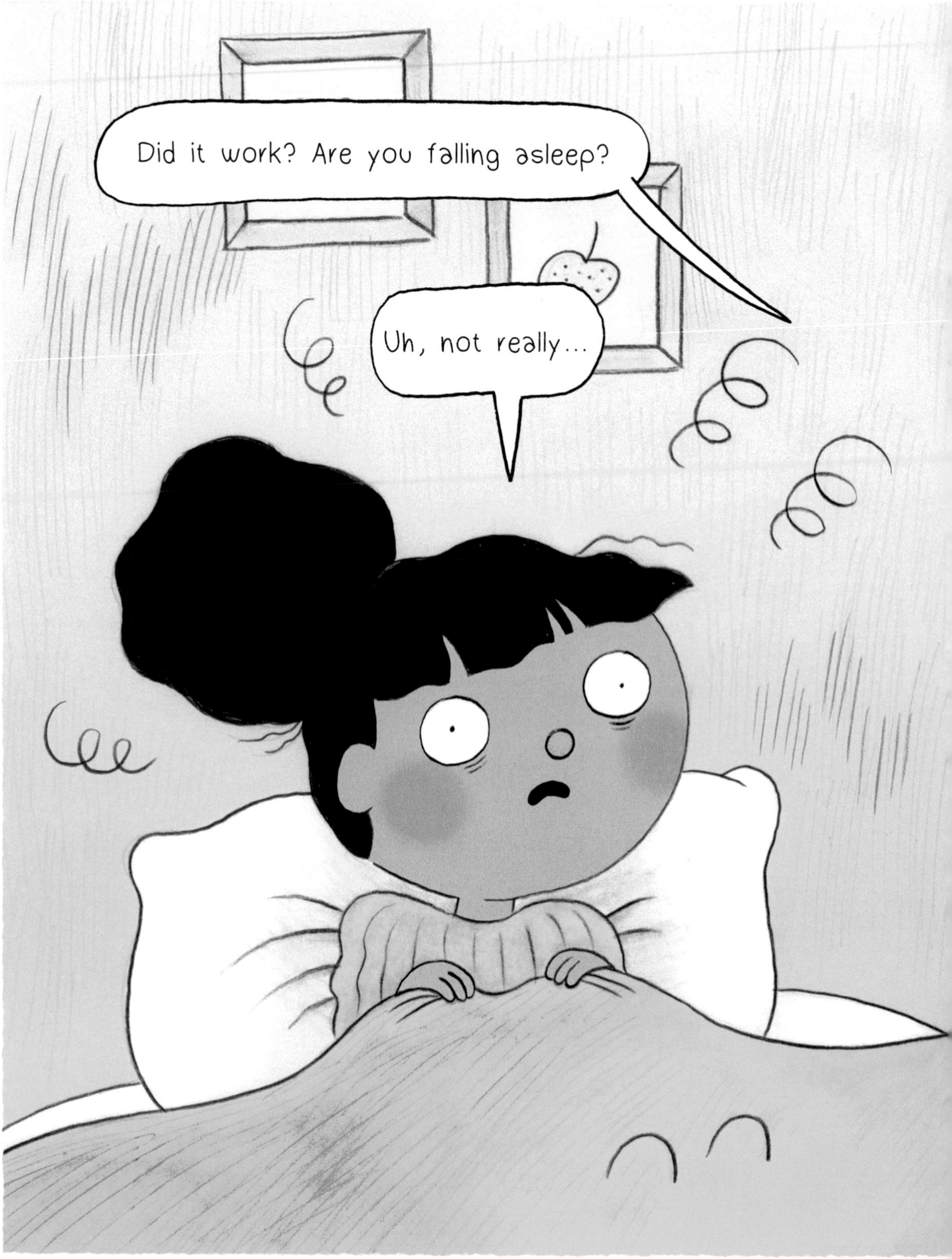
Did it work? Are you falling asleep?
Uh, not really...

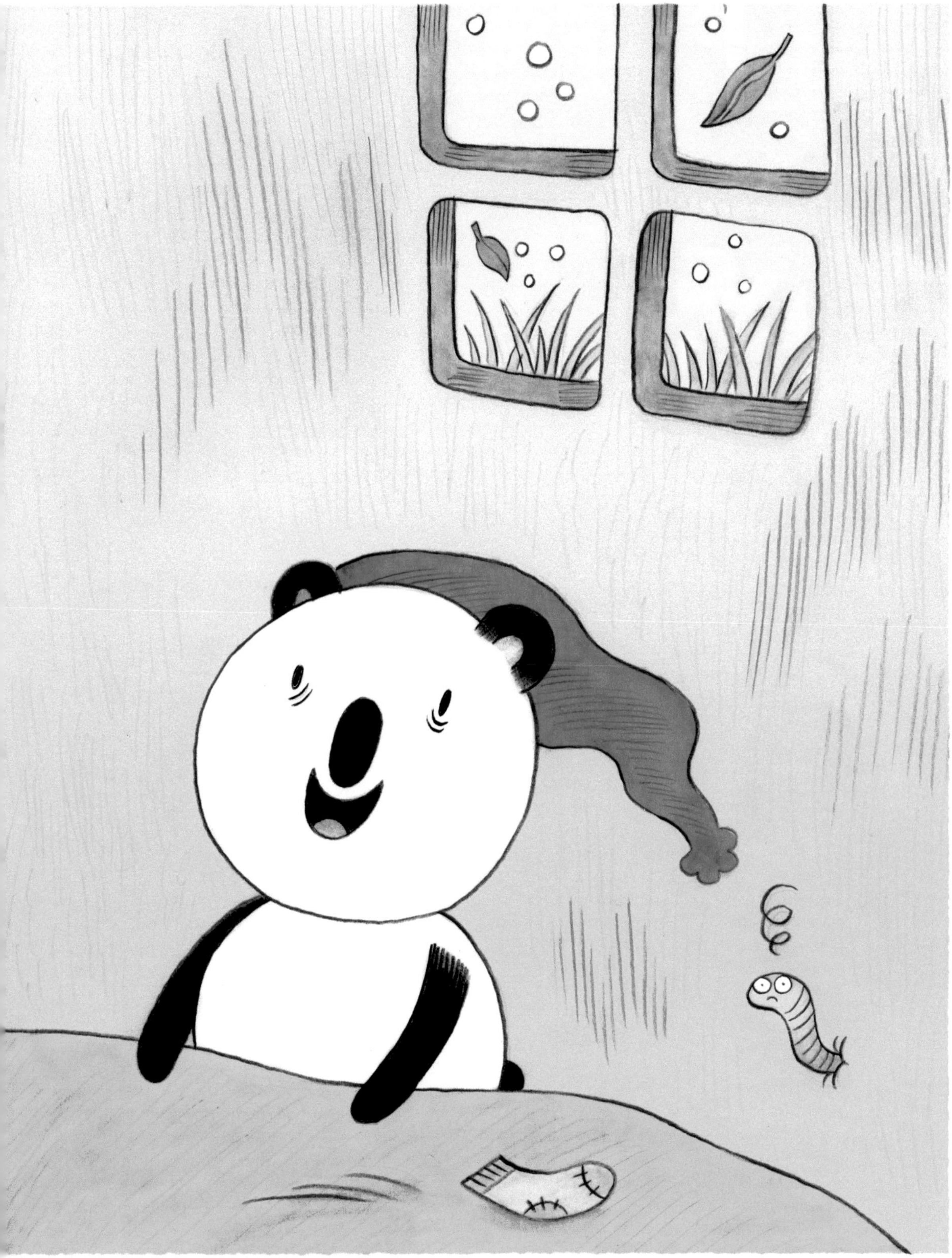

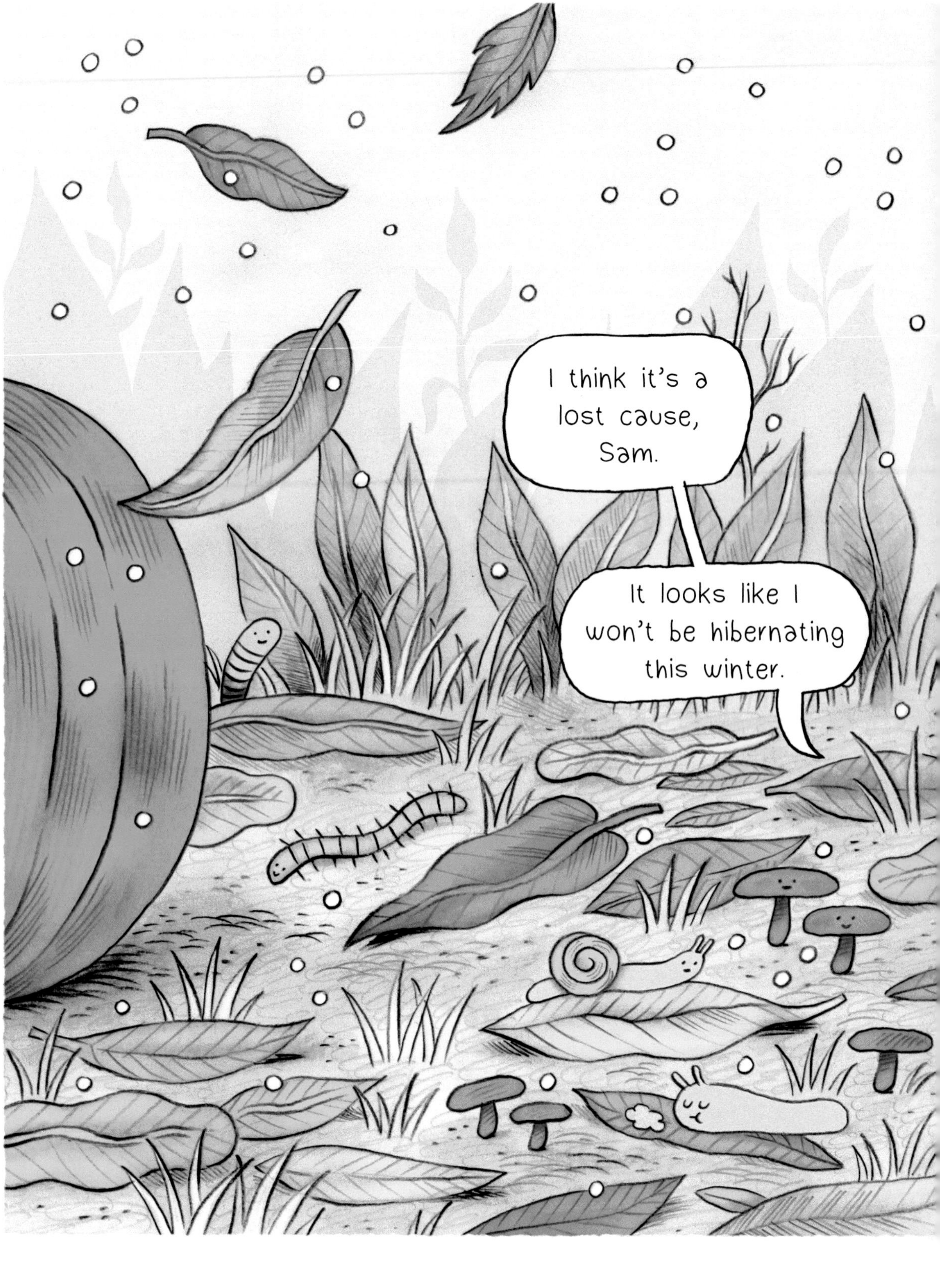
I think it's a lost cause, Sam.
It looks like I won't be hibernating this winter.

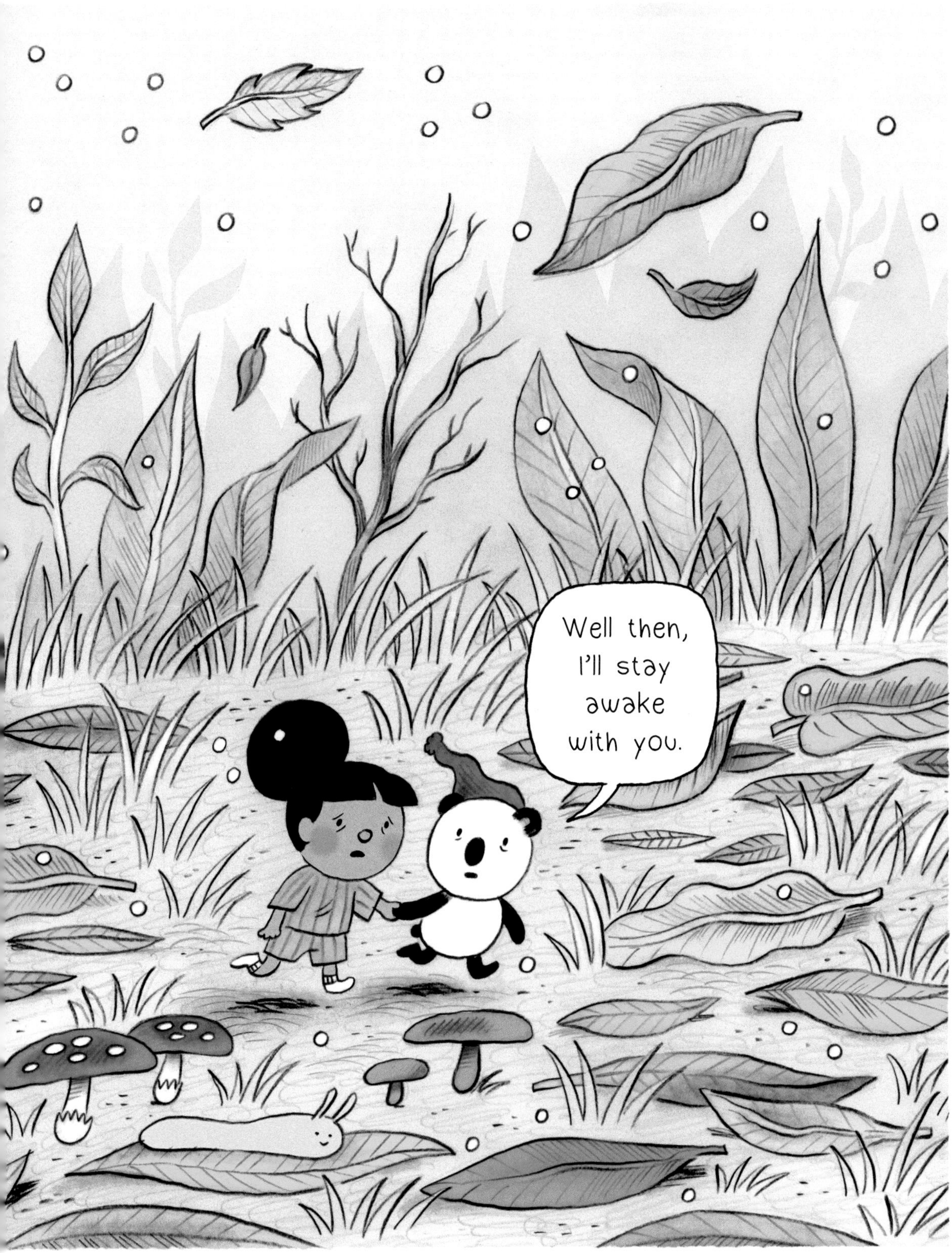
Well then, I'll stay awake with you.

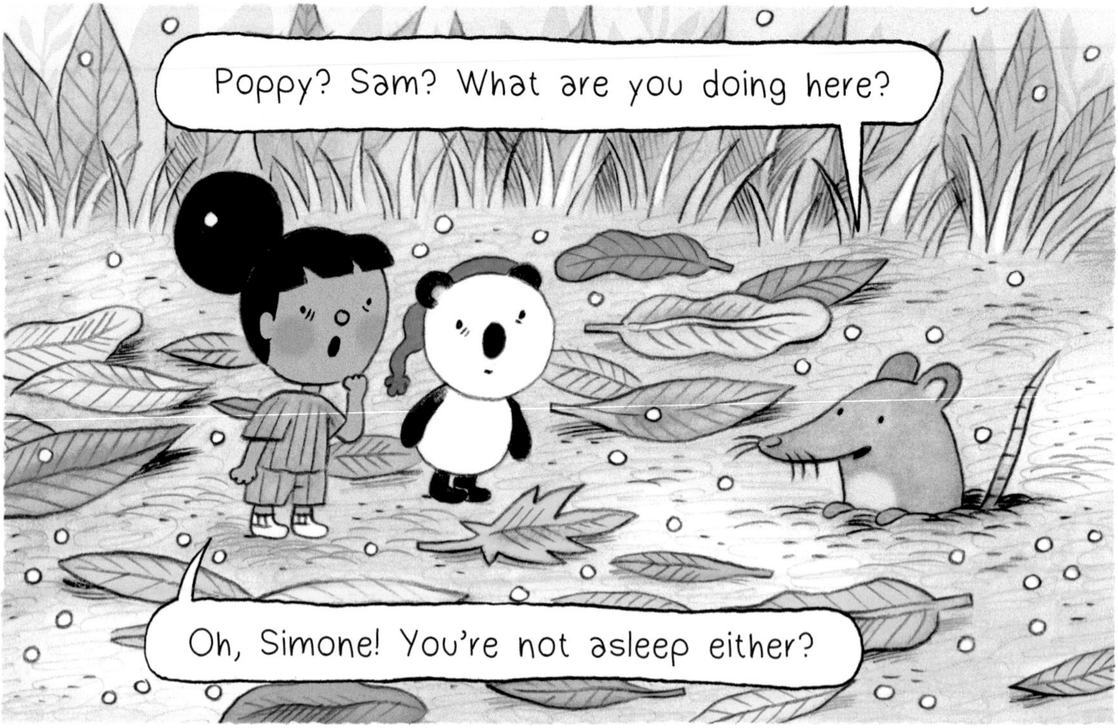
Poppy? Sam? What are you doing here?
Oh, Simone! You're not asleep either?

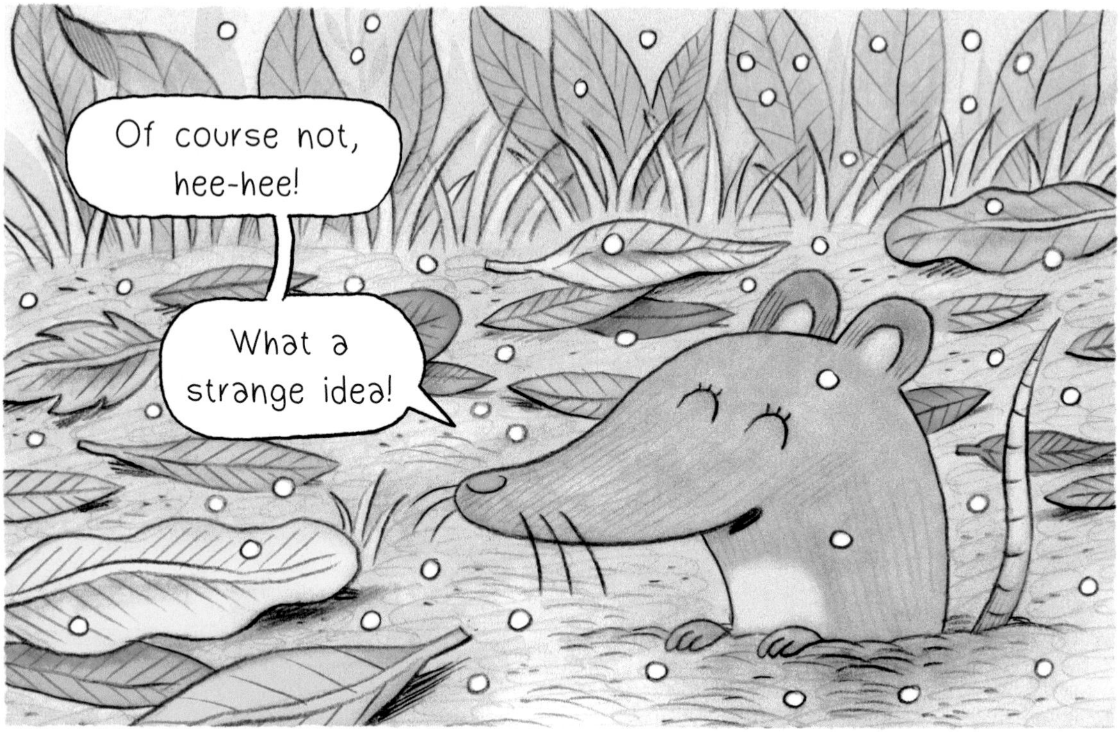
Of course not, hee-hee!
What a strange idea!

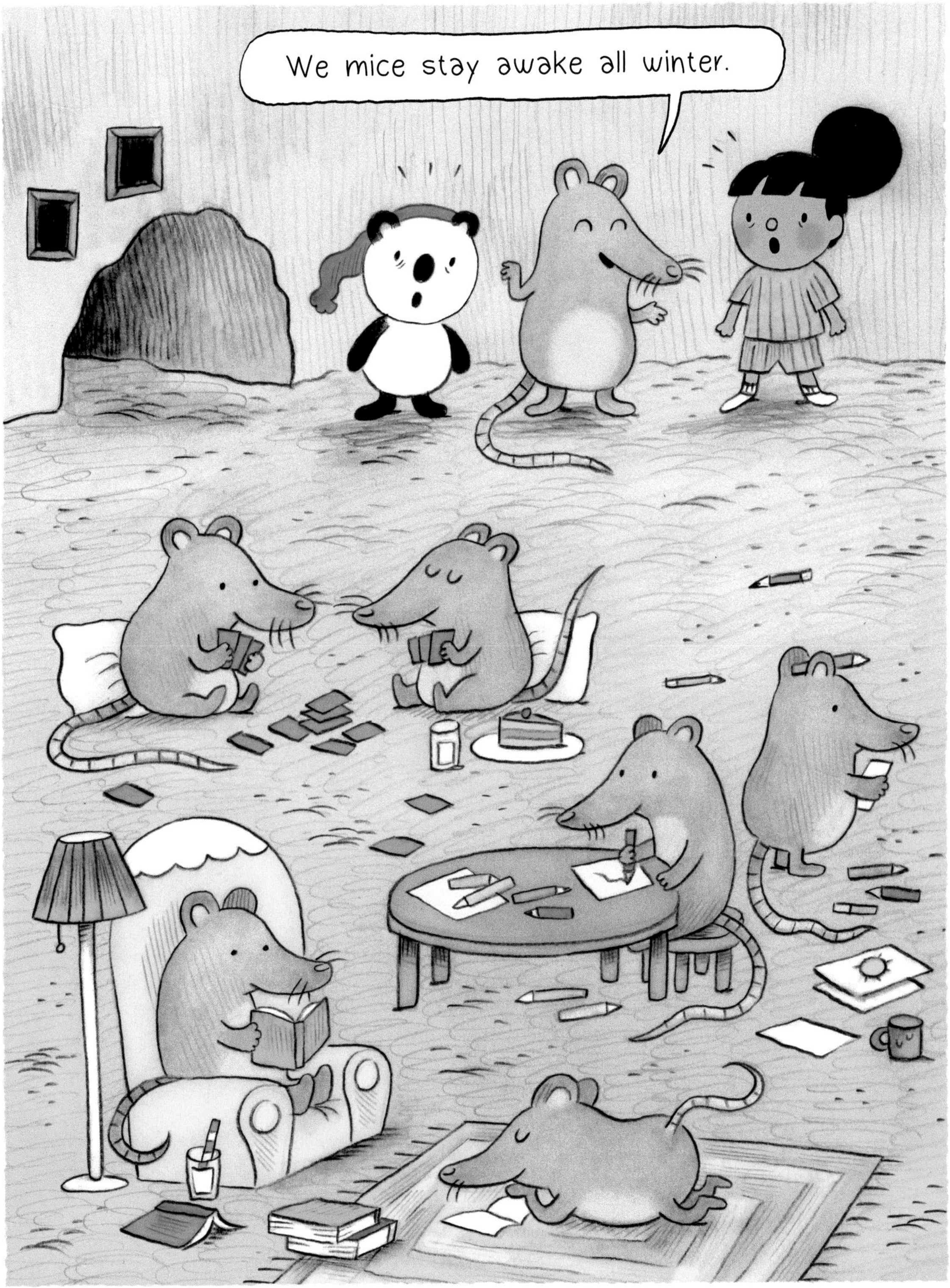
We mice stay awake all winter.

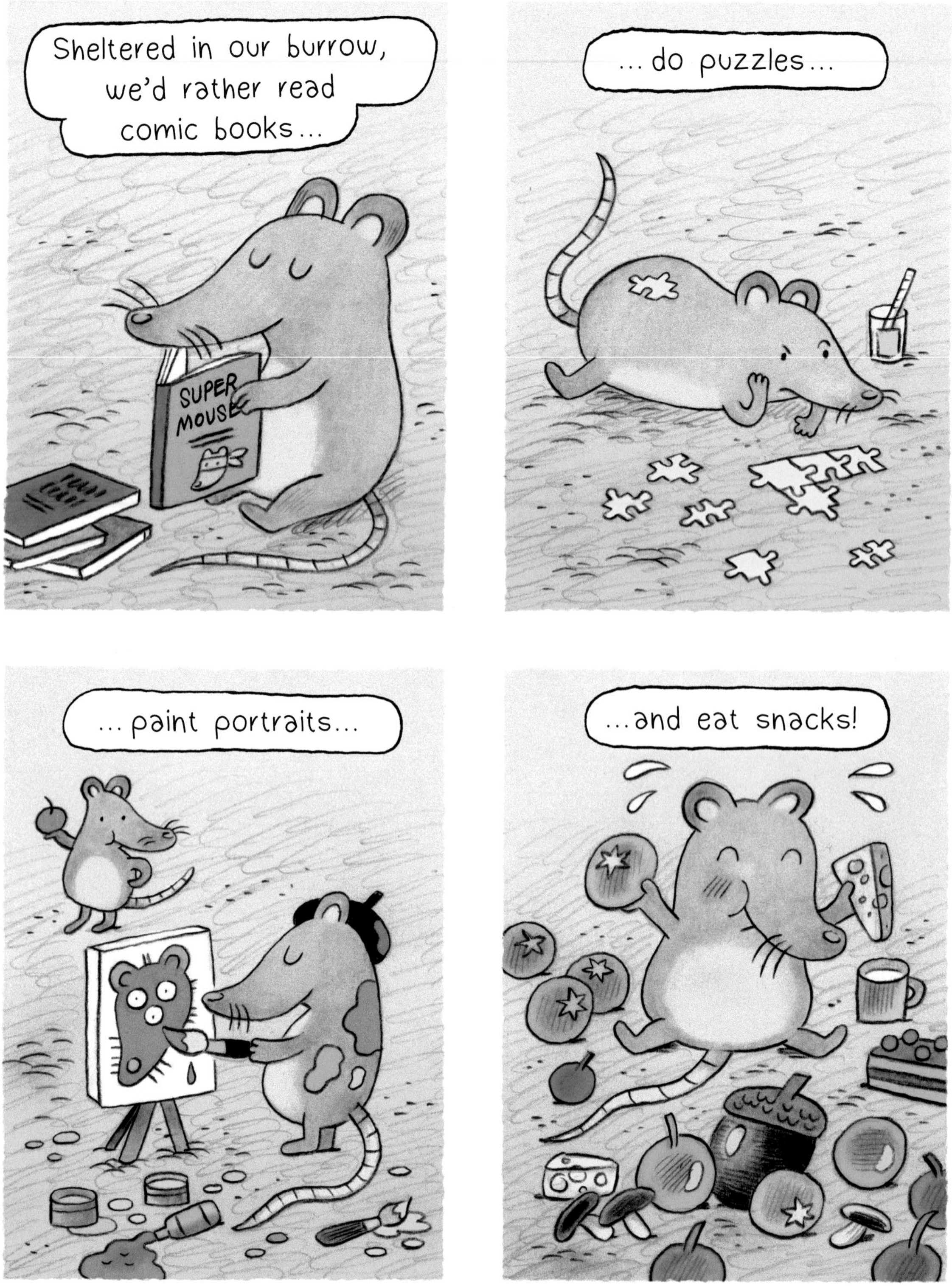
Sheltered in our burrow, we'd rather read comic books...
SUPER MOUSE
... do puzzles...
... paint portraits...
...and eat snacks!

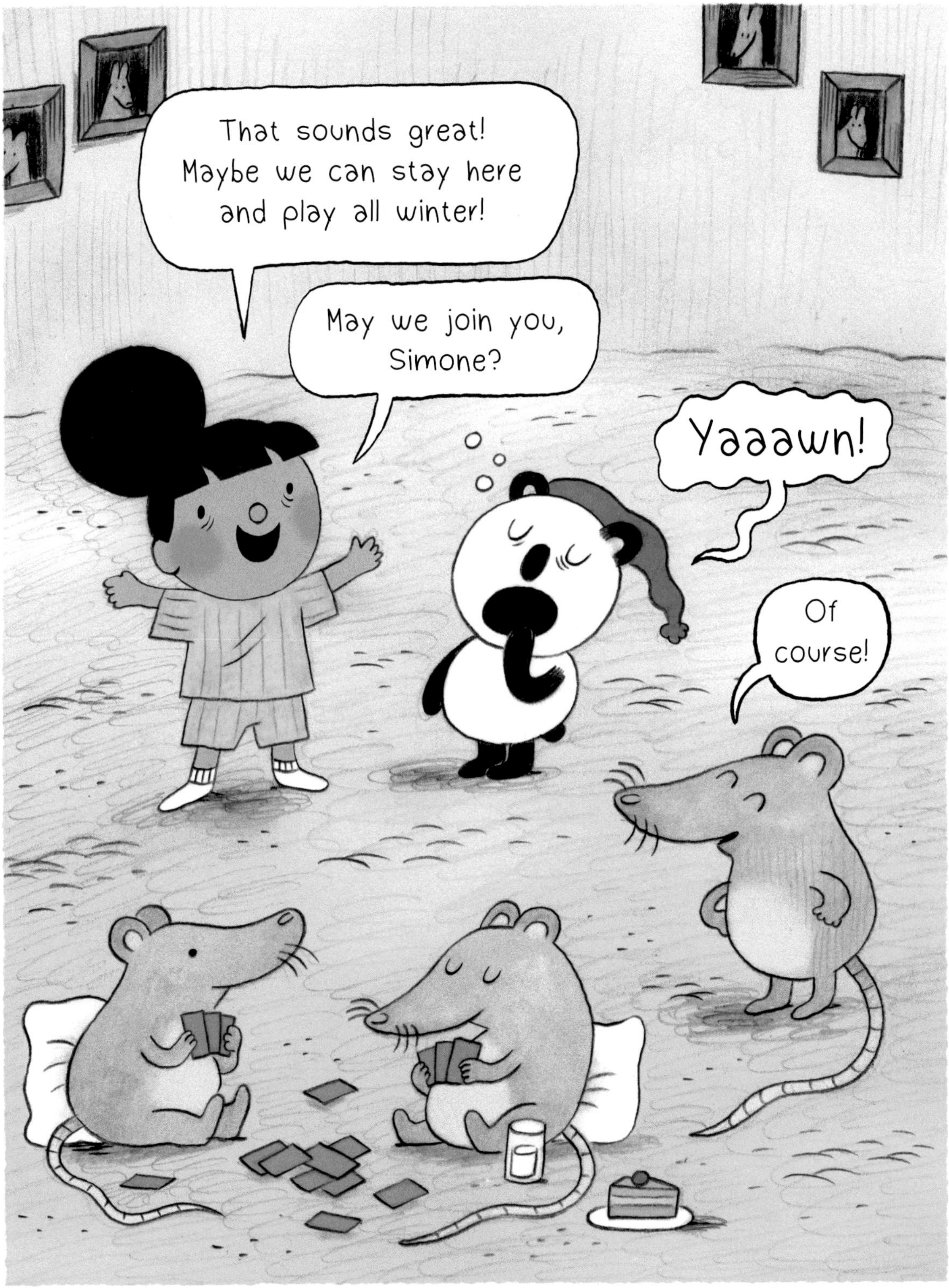
That sounds great! Maybe we can stay here and play all winter!
May we join you, Simone?
Yaaawn!
Of course!

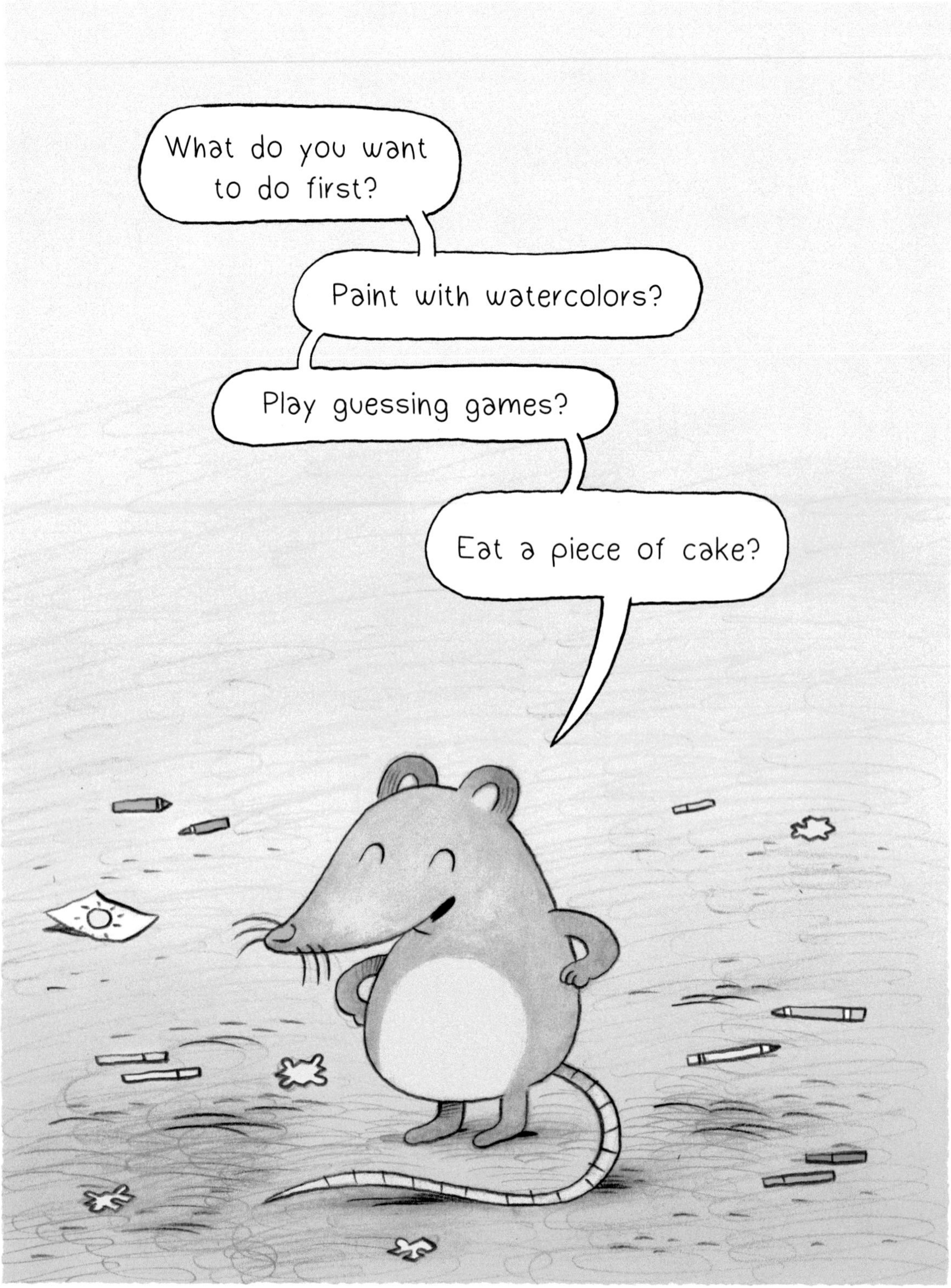
What do you want to do first?
Paint with watercolors?
Play guessing games?
Eat a piece of cake?

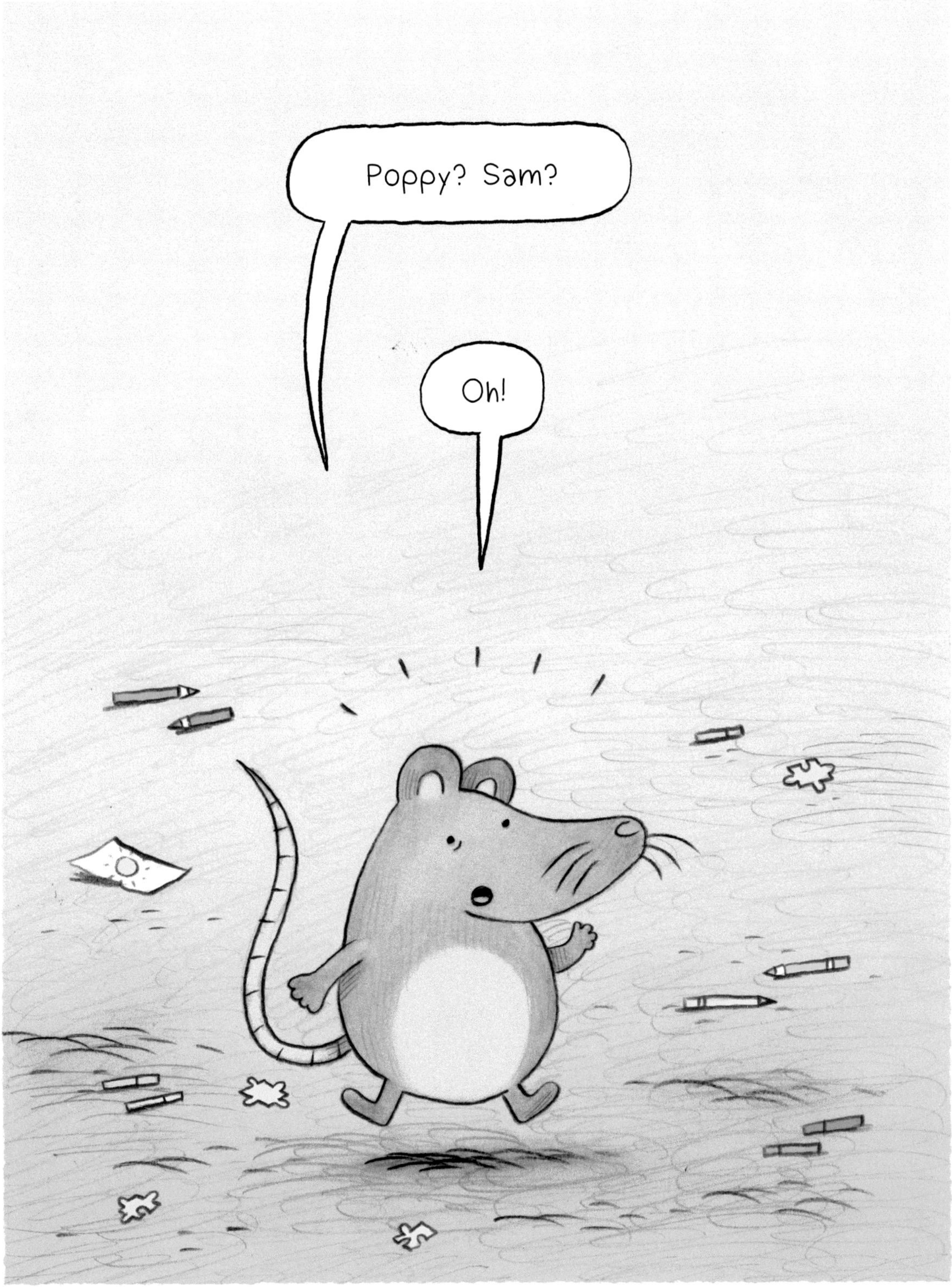
Poppy? Sam?
Oh!

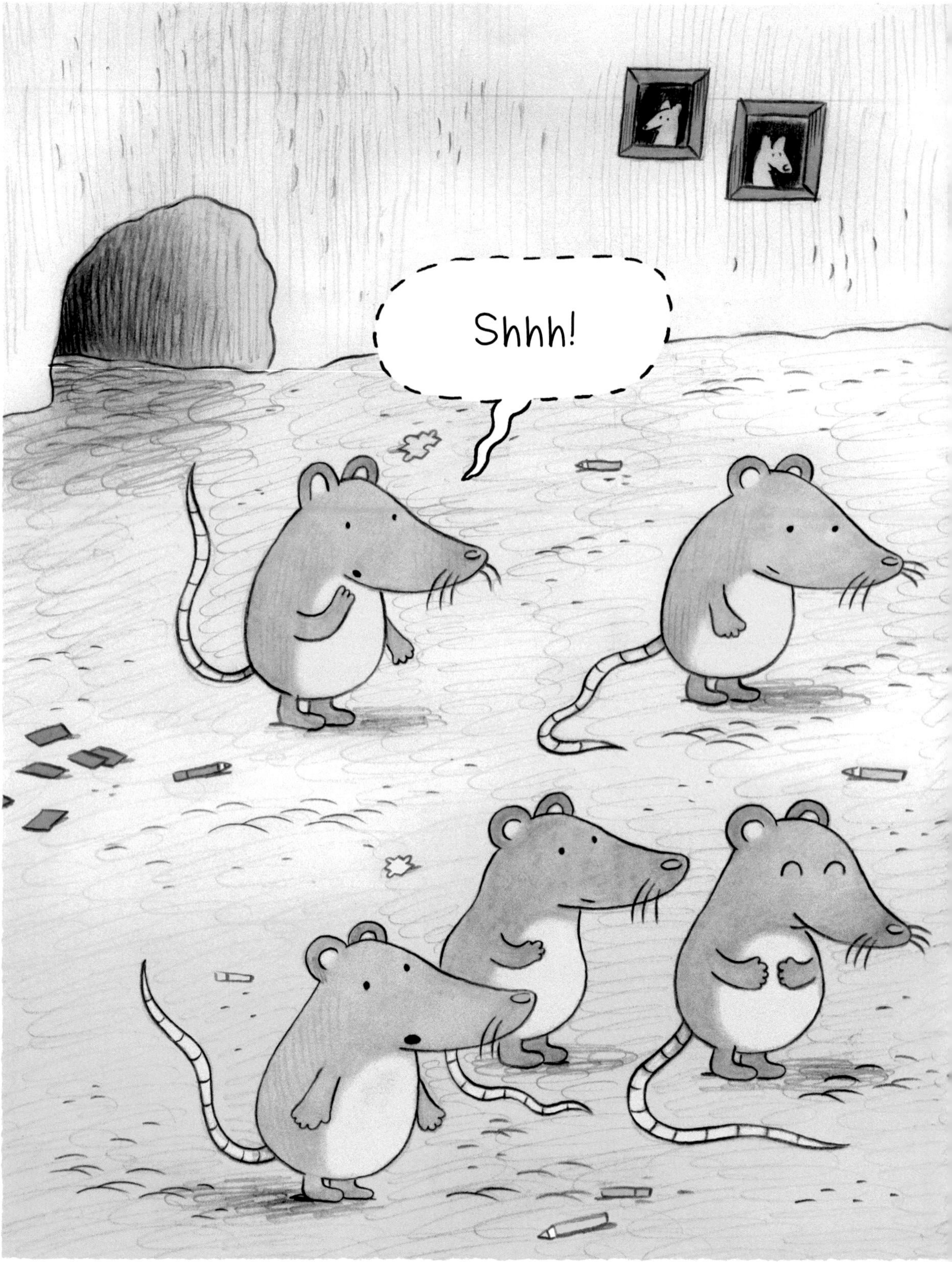
Shhh!

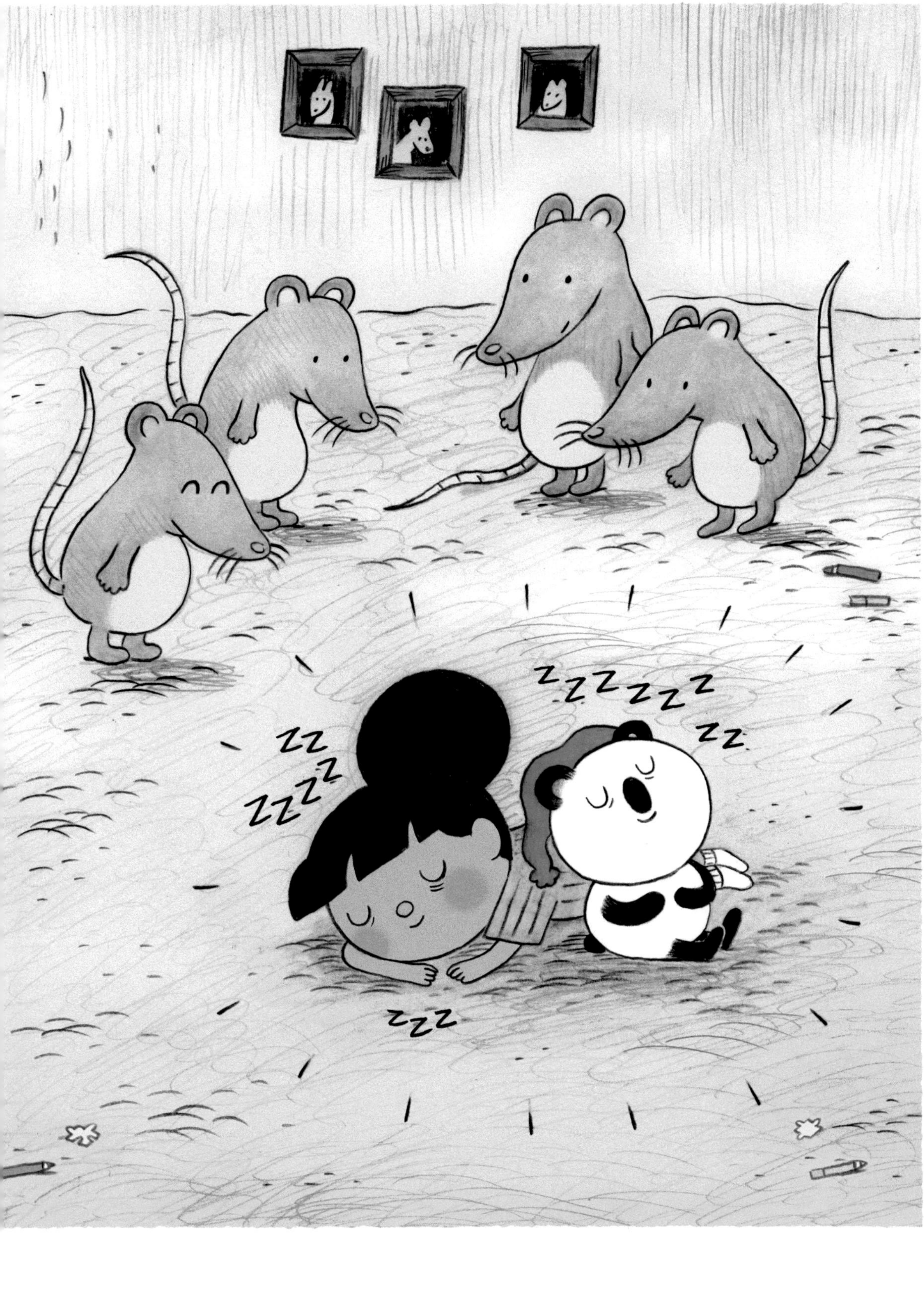
ZZZZZZZ
ZZ
ZZ
ZZZZZ
ZZZ

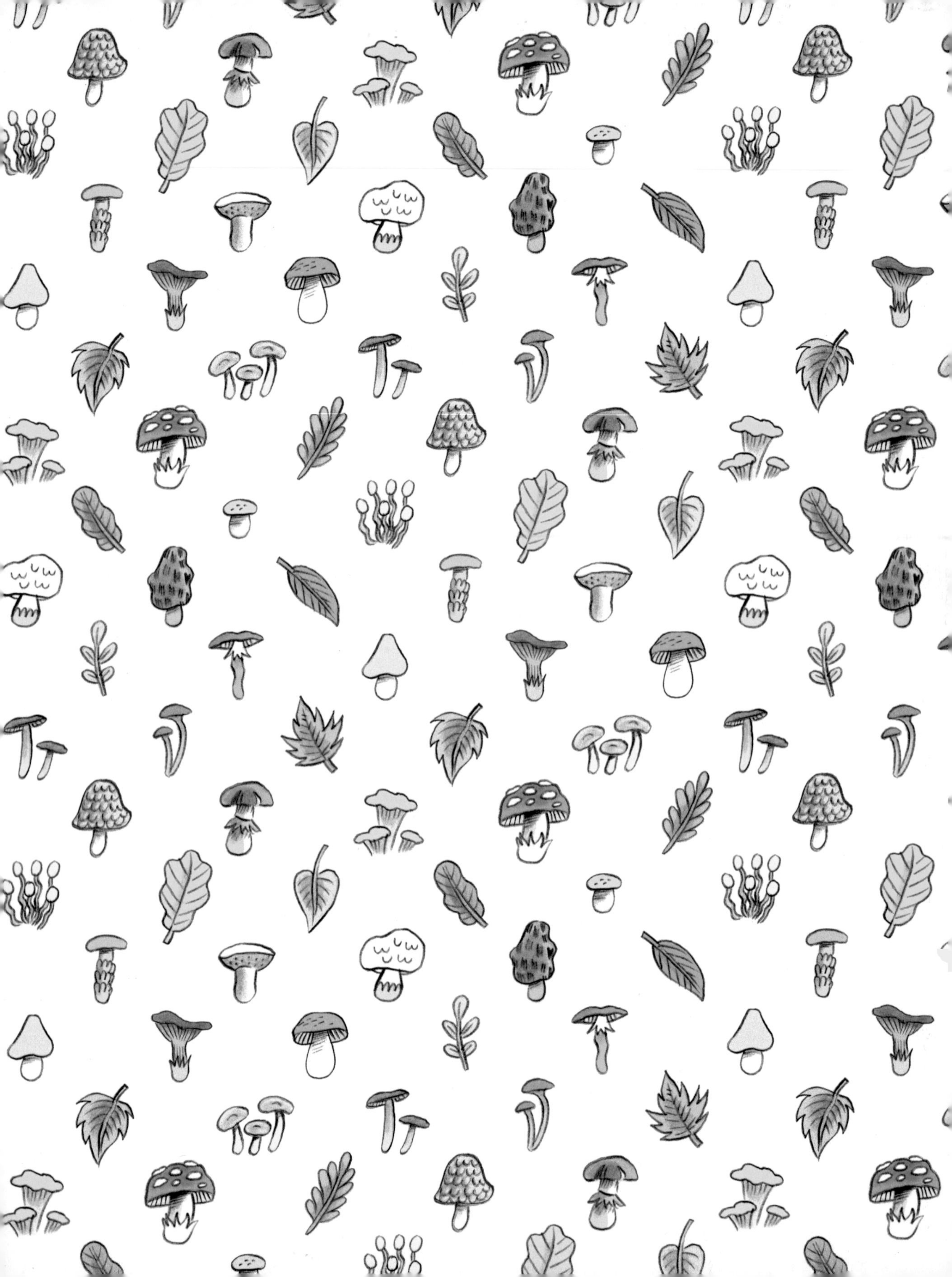